THE TIME OF THE KRAKEN

THE TIME
OF
THE
KRAKEN

by Jay Williams

VICTOR GOLLANCZ LTD
LONDON
1978

Printed in Great Britain by
Lowe & Brydone Printers Limited, Thetford, Norfolk

CONTENTS

THE TIME OF THE KRAKEN

I

THE RUNNER

ON this day, the Loosing of the Waters, life began again. Or at any rate, that was how Thorgeir Redhair put it to himself, watching among the other young men and women from the top of the slope.

It was partly the holiday air: almost the whole town of Velir spread out along the sides of the hill, wearing their best clothing, the bright-dyed kirtles and smocks like a shifting garden when the wind blows over it. Some munched bread and sausages, chattering with greasy faces. Children played mysterious games underfoot, and parents smacked their heads casually to make them behave, without pausing in their talk. Old men, wagging their beards, remarked that the weather and the crop were not what they had been in the old days. And among the youths, their weapons laid aside, there was horseplay and laughter and flirtation.

And the cause of it all lay stretched out before them along

the valley, acre upon acre of the new selva waiting for the water. What only a day or so ago had been the stripes of hard, pebbly furrows were now blurred with tender green. It was, Thorgeir thought, like magic, like the old fairy tales, like the saga of Budri Brightface, this appearance from nowhere of the young leaves that meant bread in their mouths for another year. Not only bread which was ground from the seed-heads; the seed could be fermented for beer or pressed for oil, the root was delicious baked or boiled, and the stems, soaked, stripped and beaten, could be woven into cloth. No wonder that even among the Detestable People, the Tyrnings, the day on which the first shoots appeared and the irrigation channels must be opened was celebrated as it was among the villages and towns of the Vollings.

Hlod Erni's-son, a grin on his flat, freckled face, said, "Someone has been looking for you."

"Who?" asked Thorgeir, before he thought, and then understood and blushed.

"I told her you said you didn't want to see her any more. Did I do well?"

"Wonderfully well. And you will do still better when your mouth is stuffed with sand."

He was embarrassed but not really angry. It was too fine a day for that. He made a halfhearted grab at Hlod, who skipped out of reach, laughing.

"Disease and destruction," said a thin, beaky-nosed lad, clapping Thorgeir on the back. It was a current joke among them to twist the customary greeting, "Health to you," out of shape. "Where is your brother? I haven't seen him since the raid, and he's not here now."

"No," Thorgeir answered. "He was sent on some errand by our father, something secret."

"Yes, something is going on," said Hlod. "None of the councillors are here for the Loosing. What are they discussing?"

Thorgeir shook his head. His attention was elsewhere. He was looking for a sight of Ylga among the crowd.

Over the brow of the hill, from the direction of the town, banners appeared. A stir went through the watching people, a final burst of noise, warning hushes, exclamations: "They are coming! Stand still. Be quiet, Sturla!" Then came four men with spears, the blades wreathed with sprigs of selva made of beaten gold, and among them a fifth man walking slowly, old Ari Flatnose, one of the priests of Arveid.

As Thorgeir watched, a hand was put into his. He turned in startlement, and smiled when he saw who it was.

Ylga's brown eyes were almost on a level with his. Her smooth brown hair was braided huntress-fashion in a coronet about her head. She wore a blue-dyed kirtle embroidered with flying tree-mice about the hem and collar. Her cheeks were flushed with excitement, and he thought he had never seen her look prettier.

"Here you are," she said.

"Here I am. And here you are. I've been looking for you."

"You haven't been looking very hard. I have seen you standing on this same spot for hours."

He reddened. "If you've been watching me all that time, why didn't you come sooner, then?" he retorted.

She squeezed his hand. "You are too quick witted for me. How can you bear anyone as slow and stupid as I am?"

"Stop teasing, Ylga."

"Does it make you uncomfortable? You are thin skinned, too."

He looked imploringly at her, but said nothing. She took pity on him, smiling at him, the tall, lithe, red-haired boy with a long, homely, but strong-boned face and, oddly, eyes that did not quite match, one gray-green, the other gray-blue. That was only one of the oddities that had first attracted her to him. He had a hot temper which he kept in check, showing instead a mildness of manner which kept him out of those quarrels and duels so natural to most young warriors. In raids, he had been known to weep over a fallen foe. And most curiously, he did not share everyone else's hatred of the Detestable People, the followers of the false Arveid, nor was he ever heard to speak ill of them. It was an independence of thinking which had caused some of the others to shake their heads over him. But as for her, she liked a man who could hold to his own opinion.

She said, softly, "Tomorrow, I am going hunting alone for small game. I will go into Vapnwood beyond the Long Stone. Wouldn't it be an interesting surprise if we met each other on the way?"

He nodded, unable to reply.

"Be quiet, they're beginning," she said, severely. "How can I hear what Ari says if you talk so much?"

Ari now stood on the flat Overseer's Stone, a short way down from the top of the hill. His bodyguard ranked behind him. To his left lay a crest of ribbed rock forming a rim along the top of the selva fields; to his right, all along the hillslope were the people. Two hundred paces from the Overseer's Stone was the sluice gate, with four men standing ready at the ropes that raised it. On the other side of the rocky crest was the reservoir, centuries old, built by the first settlers, fed by three lucky springs which had never yet run dry.

Ari wore a white robe without sleeves, and on his shriveled wrists were bracelets of gold which flashed as he raised his arms.

One of the bodyguards, in a loud voice, cried, "I call you all to witness! Listen, and be still!"

In the dead silence, the faint breeze could be heard whispering among the thin weeds on the hill. And Ari said, in his hoarse but carrying voice, "Arveid, Goddess, Golden Maiden, all praise to You. Hail, bright-haired Skyborn One, from whose hand we accept earth's bounty, to whom we shall one day return in peace."

A murmur came from the crowd, "Hail, Maiden."

"Daughter of Udi, You who taught us to plant the selva, to nurture it, to harvest it, to use its—"

He stopped. Thorgeir felt Ylga's fingers grip his arm. People were pointing. In the distance, a tiny speck had appeared.

Thorgeir shaded his eyes as many were doing. A man was running at full speed along the narrow road from Esk and Imma and the villages of the north. Closer he came, tiny plumes of dust trailing at his heels, his legs and arms pumping, his head high. Now he was upon the stone causeway that crossed the selva fields on many arches over the irrigation channels. Even at that distance, Thorgeir recognized his elder brother.

"It's Athils," he said.

"Where has he been?" said Ylga.

Thorgeir shrugged. The runner was near enough so that others now knew him, and a buzz of talk arose. Athils crossed the last span of the causeway and ran up the hill. His face was streaming with sweat and set in the kind of trance of extreme exertion which warriors were trained to induce, and which they called "breathborn." Looking neither to one side nor the other, Athils ran up the hill, the crowd parting to let him through. He vanished over the brow.

"Blast and be damned!" said Ari, clearly. Now that the ceremony had been interrupted, it had to be begun again from the beginning.

"I call you all to witness," shouted the bodyguard, once more.

Hlod Erni's-son, standing behind Thorgeir, muttered, "A bad omen. It's unlucky to break off the rite."

"Don't be so superstitious," said Ylga, over her shoulder.

"An omen of something," Thorgeir said, thoughtfully. "He was sent in secret and he comes back in haste."

"Maybe a battle," said thin Rolf, on Thorgeir's left. "May it be so. I am too young to be so bored."

"—in Your name, I loose the waters," said Ari.

He dropped his arms. The four men hauled; the sluice gate rose, creaking, and sparkling brown water poured out. It filled the upper trenches quickly and purled down the channels. The green leaves now lay in strips of sky.

Ari chanted the first line of the Plea to Arveid, and the people began to sing it. Thorgeir, who had no ear for music, stood mute listening to Ylga's pure, clear contralto, when someone tapped him on the shoulder.

It was one of his father's kemperymen, who guarded the Speaker's back in battle and acted as his servants in peace. "Come to the council hall at once," he whispered. "You are wanted."

When Frodi Heavyhand, Chief Speaker of the Council of the Vollings summoned, few people waited, least of all his sons. Thorgeir turned to Ylga and said, "I must go." Too shy to kiss her openly, he raised her hand halfway to his lips, and dropped it.

"Tomorrow," she said.

He hastened after the kemperyman. On the other side of the hill lay the town of Velir, a sprawl of wooden houses, reed-thatched or shingled, each with its bit of garden, all the shutters wide to the spring breeze. It was strange to pass through unpeopled lanes and look into empty houses, empty booths and workshops, to cross a deserted marketplace, with all the folk who could walk at the Loosing of the Waters. On the other side of the town lay the open field where the Assembly was held, and to one side of it was the small, plain wooden hall where the council met, with the Swearing Stone of Udi before its doors. Even as he approached it, Thorgeir could hear a loud voice raised in angry speech.

He entered as unobtrusively as he could, and stood in a corner near the door where his father could see him. At the round table sat the five councillors, and behind his father stood Athils, his shirt sticking to his body, still wet from his running. He alone took any notice of Thorgeir and grinned at him across the room. Two years older, he was also taller than Thorgeir, broader in chest and shoulder, built more like their father, Frodi, and with the same wide-cheeked, wide-nostrilled face. The red hair he, like Thorgeir, had from their mother was darker, nearly brown, although his beard was light.

It was Svip Leaper who was speaking, pounding on the table for emphasis. Nothing was left of the agility that had once given him his name, for he was thick and fat, his neck bulging over the links of a heavy gold chain.

"And must we sit and bear it in silence?" he shouted. "Because the Speaker says that all will be well? We have born it too long already, far too long, the attacks of those heretical outlaws, the insolence of those enemies of the Goddess! Did they not burn up Osmun's steading and Osmun and his wife and children inside it? Wasn't it they who began the bloodshed at the Midyear Market? I say that if we sit mum now, they will be moving in with us next, in Velir, ousting us from our own homes—''

''Be calm, Svip, we do not wish to see you fall dead from anger,'' said Bera Agni's-daughter, mockingly. She was a tall, darkly handsome woman, hawk nosed, fierce of eye. She spoke lazily, but with an edge to her voice. ''I, for one, do not—''

''You will always stand with Frodi, we know that,'' sneered Svip.

''I have not yet said what I think, so be still.'' He sat back, growling. ''In the matter of raids, we are not altogether blameless. But that is not the question. I am not ready to see the whole world burst into red war because a handful of them have moved into the hill land above Nimma's Field. That is debatable land, never claimed by either side. At the very least, let us try what talking can do before we draw the sword.''

''And I say—'' Svip began, but the deep voice of the Speaker broke in upon him.

''You have already spoken, and twice,'' said Frodi. ''Is this a council or a squabbling of children? We will hear others, first.''

Taller by half a head than anyone there was Frodi, shaggy and huge, his black hair showing no more than a thread or two of gray. The knobby bones of his cheeks made his eyes seem small, but they were piercing, and although his tone was quiet he dominated Svip.

''Now, Jodrunn, we have heard nothing from you,'' he

went on, turning to a thin, fair woman who sat with her elbow on the table, her chin resting in her palm.

She bent forward, looking at the tabletop. On it was drawn a map of all the known world. From north to south ran the jagged spine of the mountains, Blackfell Ridge and Baldrock, the twin points of Hugin and Munin, Boldneb, the Pass of Voll, mighty peaks and spires. To the west was the land of the Tyrnings, its southwestern part lying upon the Brine Lake with its rich salt pans. To the east was Vollingsland, bounded by the vast forest of Vapn and, in the north, the heights of Nimma's Field, a cold and barren plateau. Below that part, in the foothills, lay the town of Esk with its mines, the wealth of the Vollings. Southward was the Sea which none had yet crossed; in the far north, the wild waste called the Meadow of Arveid lay.

A while Jodrunn studied this map, and then she said, musingly, "I see one danger."

"Aha!" said Svip.

She glanced at him. "Let me say, first, that I agree with the Speaker. 'Foot follows foot,' as the saying goes. I do not wish to take steps toward war if they can be avoided, and first we must try what bargaining can do. But I do not like to see Tyrnings settled here"—she touched the map with one finger—"only a mile or less from the edge of Nimma's Field and so only a short distance from Esk, and the mines."

The remaining councillor, a man with a bland, round, merry face, now far from merry, shook his head. He was called

Ragn the Peacemaker. He said, "True, true. If it were I who led them, I would swoop down suddenly, burn the town and seize the mines. Who holds the mines, holds the Vollingfolk to ransom."

"There, by the Eye of Udi!" cried Svip. "That is what I meant. If we are not swift to act we shall find ourselves bonded and bound, forced to kiss the foot of their High Priest and swear that the Devil Arveid is our Goddess. Do they not use the blood of babies as a sacrifice? Are we to give up our children to them? Or are we to be traitors to our religion and our people?"

Ragn touched his knuckles to the table. "May it not be so. But Svip, consider—are the people of Velir to go out to battle without the rest of the Vollings? Or would you have Frodi call for war without asking for a vote? I don't know much, but I know what our folk are like. No one commands a Volling, you might as well command the birds to stop singing. You yourself were born in Havarda. Surely it is said, 'Hardheaded as a Hverding'? We have had the proof of it today."

The others chuckled and even Svip grinned. The tension eased. Then Frodi put in, with a hard look at Svip, "I do not think we have any traitors here. I think we are all agreed that something must be done, and Ragn has shown us what it is. We must first call the High Moot together. Messengers must go at once to every town and village with the summons, and let it be in five days that all the councillors meet here in Velir. When we have laid the case before them, we can take the first step toward arbitration with the Tyrnings. And after that, if they will not hear us, let there be talk of war. But I leave it all to the Moot."

His gaze gathered them in. "Are we so agreed?"

"I think we are," said Ragn. He looked at Svip, who nodded.

"And," added Bera, "let it be said that this council gives its thanks to Athils Frodi's-son for his report to us."

They all drummed their fists on the table, and Athils, hands on hips, bowed, smiling with downcast eyes.

They rose with a scrape of stools, and Jodrunn said, "It is near noon and the people are at their feasting for the holiday. My rede is that we keep this news to ourselves for now, and let the messengers be sent out before daybreak tomorrow, when they will be fresh and will not grumble at losing their dinners. I will choose the runners, if you like."

Svip had gone to clap Athils on the shoulder. "A daredevil!" he said. "Just such as I was when I was young. By Udi's spear, that was a bold deed and a good run."

"I had rather see the Tyrnings run," said Athils. "And me behind them."

"Well said. You are the next war captain we choose, if I have my way," said Svip.

Athils replied, modestly, "I will serve in any way I am asked."

When the councillors had gone, Frodi gripped Athils by the shoulder.

"I thank you, too, my son," he said. "It was well done from the start. Now go, bathe and change your clothes, and have your dinner. I have something to say to Thorgeir and then we will join you."

Athils stroked his dense, short beard. "Will there be war?"

"It is for the High Moot to decide."

Athils looked narrowly at his father. "You can sway them. When were you ever overborne? If you wish it, they will go where you lead. And surely Jodrunn was right and there is real danger? Even Ragn saw that."

"I do not yet know what I wish," said Frodi, frowning. "Nor is it true that I was never overborne. I am the Speaker, not a king nor a tyrant. Do not forget that, Athils."

There was iron in his tone, and Athils, although still looking defiant, bent his head. More gently, Frodi went on, "I know *your* wish, at any rate. It is for glory in battle. A good wish for a youth, but remember not all the Vollings are warriors. Go, now."

When Athils had gone, not without looking back in curiosity, Frodi turned to Thorgeir, who had stood all this while silent in his corner. The Speaker's eyes were soft. In the face of his younger son, he saw the features of his wife dead these five years, and besides there was in Thorgeir something that touched his father closely, gentleness without weakness, which sounded an answering note in Frodi's heart.

After a moment, he said, "Come and sit down."

As Thorgeir seated himself on one of the stools, Frodi looked outside the door of the hall and sent away his kemperyman who still waited there. Then he returned, to sit beside his son.

"You heard all that was said?" he asked.

"Yes, I heard."

"You understood?"

"Some of the Tyrnings have settled in Nimma's Field, above Esk. How did you learn of it?"

"It was Athils' doing. He is perhaps overfond of fighting, but in this case it was all to the good. You will remember that he took a small band some weeks ago over the northern pass at Boldneb and raided some of the steadings near Breita. He was pursued and fled back over the pass and rested at Imma, for one of his men was badly hurt. While there, a herder told him the rumor that people had been glimpsed up on the high ground. Wisely, he did not leave his band, nor did he say anything to them. When he returned, he told me. I sent him back to scout, with orders to return this morning if he could. He has within him what will make a good war captain some day, although . . ."

He fell silent, nor did Thorgeir press him, for he knew what his father was thinking. Athils' weakness was his joy in battle, which often blinded him to all other considerations.

At last, Frodi, as if answering his son's silence, said, "We should not shrink from war, but we should not desire it. Do you desire it, Thorgeir?"

"I hate it," he said, simply.

Frodi nodded. "I know you are no coward. But if war were to come?"

"I will put my hand to whatever must be. But life is too good to wish for anyone's death."

"Not even an unbeliever's?"

Thorgeir hesitated. Then he said, "Arveid is the Life-bringer. Did she not give the selva to all of us, even the Tyrnings?"

"Yes," said Frodi. He added, "It has not been easy for you, sometimes, my son, to stand against the stream."

"Oh, I have been called stink-lover and other names," said Thorgeir, with a half smile. "Yet I can find no wound they made on me. Even Athils . . ."

"Your brother loves popularity. I do not blame him for what he is. There is much of me in him."

Thorgeir's chin lifted. "I never heard you call the Tyrnings by any name other than that. You have never called them the Detestable Ones. Nor my mother—"

"Your mother hated no one." Frodi sighed, turning this way and that the massive gold bracelet that clasped his wrist. "And as for me, I have a blood brother among them."

Thorgeir stared. "Among the Tyrnings?"

"Just so." He clasped his hands together, and looked down at his hairy knuckles. In a low voice, he continued, "It was many years ago, when I was Athils' age, twenty, and like him a great brawler and bickerer. I had led eleven raids and had fought six duels, in one of them wounding my man so badly that my father had to pay a heavy ransom. Your grandfather, Thorkil, was a man slow to heat but once roused, of furious temper. He knocked me across the room and then told me that I had better get out of his sight for a while. So I took some provisions and went into the mountains.

"I went among the foothills of the south, to Blackfell Ridge, where I had never been. There is a way there into Tyrningsland and I had it in my mind that if I grew bored I would have some sport among their outlying villages. I lived among the hills for several days, going down to the forest to hunt, for there is a great wood there which runs for many miles southward to the Sea. Once, down there, I saw an ylvan."

Thorgeir's eyes widened. The ylvan were almost legendary; great beasts, eaters of leaves it was said, glimpsed but seldom in only the thickest woods, never harmful to mankind—so far as anyone knew, and that was little. Stories were told of how they had helped benighted hunters, of how they could even speak with a human tongue.

"Did you speak to it?" he said.

Frodi chuckled. "I had nothing to say. Indeed, I was too frightened to mark it clearly, only that it was big. Well, on the fifth day, up on the shoulder of Blackfell, like a fool, I broke my leg."

"How did it happen?"

"There were stokkna up there." These were light-footed,

small animals that lived among crags, elusive, but when they could be caught, good eating. "I climbed up hoping to get within bowshot. It was a chance I should not have taken, being alone. I slipped and fell, luckily onto turf or I would have been shattered like an egg. I lay for a long time in great pain, thinking it might be better to take my dagger and do away with myself, for otherwise I would only die of hunger at last. And suddenly, a man appeared.

"He asked me nothing save where I was wounded, and when I told him he broke his spear and splinted my leg with it, using strips torn from his kirtle and mine. He had a bow with him and said he had seen the stokkna and had come up from the other side to try for a shot. He was wiser than I; when he saw that they had winded him, he gave up the climb. As for me, I knew that he could only have come from one place, Tyrningsland.

"I said to him, 'It will be better for you to kill me out of hand, for I am a Volling.' He replied, 'If you are eager for death, I can leave you here. Otherwise, be quiet.'

"He helped me hobble on one leg to my camp. Then he went away and fetched his own gear and made camp with me. And there he remained, nursing me, hunting for us both, bringing water and guarding me, until my leg had mended."

"I see," said Thorgeir, softly. "*I* would have sworn brotherhood with such a man. But how did he come to be there?"

"He had been outlawed for a year, for manslaying. It had

been done in hot blood, almost accidentally. Someone had taunted him and he had struck a blow with a hammer he was using, and killed the man. But at the lawsuit the provocation was proved, and so he had been given a light sentence."

Frodi examined his hands, the black hairs growing between the heavy knuckles, as if they were new to him. "I want you to go to him, now," he said.

"Go to him?" Thorgeir exclaimed, sitting up straight. "What for?"

Instead of answering directly, Frodi said, "He and I had plenty of time for talk. I learned from him that the Tyrnings are perhaps not so detestable as we think, and he learned from me that we do not kill a maiden every year at the Loosing of the Waters. Do you know what the Tyrnings preach, Thorgeir?"

"Only what everyone says—they worship a Demon Woman whom they call Arveid, and they do not believe in her Father, Udi. The other things, the offering of babies, the cursing of cattle, I think nothing but nonsense to frighten children."

"I will tell you what he told me. They hold that Arveid was sent by Udi in human form to the earth, to save mankind from starvation. They say that she brought with her the gift of the selva and that she taught us how to plant it and how to dam up waters and irrigate the fields. They say that she lived longer than other mortals, but that after two hundred years she died as a mortal woman, and her soul returned to her Father."

"Then they do not believe she was divine?"

"No. Nor, as we do, that on the day when Udi ends the earth and demands our accounting from us, we shall go to his home in heaven and become immortal. But you see, although we do not think alike, they worship Arveid in the same way we do, and with many of the same rites. And with reverence, Thorgeir, and with love. I cannot agree with them, but I cannot think they are so evil."

Thorgeir sat thoughtful, his chin in his hand, one finger stroking his soft, sparse moustache. Then he said, "If only everyone knew."

"None will listen," Frodi said, bitterly. "When I returned and tried to tell them, I was almost outlawed for my pains. There are some—Svip, for instance—who to this day, twenty-five years later, do not wholly trust me. And it was the same with Hjal when he returned to his people."

"Hjal? That was his name?"

"Hjal Broadbiter."

"If you know what happened to him, then you have seen him since."

"Yes, twice, secretly, in the forest below Blackfell. Twice in all these years! Never mind. It is a deep friendship and has survived. Listen. He is now a council member in Liskhavn and is much respected in the High Moot of his people. He is a poet and his staves are spoken widely. It may be that he does not know what is happening. Or, it may be that the settlement they have made on Nimma's Field is being done with no harmful intent, and the Tyrnings do not realize they are so close to our mines, or that hatred will rise against them.

"You must go to Hjal and tell him for me to do all he can to stop them settling there. Tell him what you heard said in the council here this morning—it is why I sent for you to be here. And make him see that if nothing is done, I cannot hold the Vollings' hands from war."

Thorgeir jumped to his feet, glowing with eagerness. "Shall I leave now?"

Frodi looked up at his son, with a warm smile. "Not without your dinner," he said.

II

AMONG THE DETESTABLE PEOPLE

GOOD as the food was which had been made for the feasting, Thorgeir ate hurriedly and little, hardly knowing what he did, his mind busy planning what he would take with him and how he would go. Frodi, at the head of the table, seemed unconcerned, jesting among his household folk, cramming gobbets of meat into his mouth, drinking great drafts from the ale horn.

Athils said softly in Thorgeir's ear, "What did our father want with you?"

Thorgeir said, as Frodi had instructed him, "It is no secret. He is sending me to watch the Pass of Voll, to see if there is any movement among the Tyrnings."

Athils grunted. "It is not the way they will come, if they come."

"Perhaps. But you know Frodi. He will take no chances."

That satisfied Athils, and he said no more.

After they had dined, the people went about their holiday

doings. There were to be games and sports, and the household chores were all left until later. Thorgeir went to his room to pack his gear, and there Frodi joined him for a moment.

"You will take the old High Road as if you are really making for the Pass," he said. "But turn off at Brekka and go cross-country to Blackfell. Skirt the forest, for although it is shorter that way it is thick and you may lose your way. Keep to the southern flanks of Blackfell and you will see a great dome of rock, like a bald head bulging out above the forest. You can cross there, and once on the other side you will find it all flat land for the most part. You saw the map. Do you remember it?"

Thorgeir nodded, tightening the drawstrings of his shoulder pack.

Frodi looked anxiously at him. "I had this in my mind when I said to the council that the Moot would assemble in five days. Five days. Can you do it?"

"It is not much further than the run Athils made, and I am lighter than he."

"But anything may happen. You are going among strangers. You must allow a whole day for rest, in Liskhavn, to be fresh for the return."

Thorgeir bit back a grin. "I know, father," he said, patiently.

Frodi set a hand on Thorgeir's shoulder. "Be careful," he said. "Not for anything would I lose you, not even if it means war."

They embraced, and Frodi left, for he wished to be seen at

the games so that he should appear untroubled. Thorgeir slung his pack on his back. He had in it only a shirt, an extra pair of shoes, a sleeping-cloth, dried provisions for two days, and a water bottle. All his weapons he left behind, save for his sword which he fastened tightly to the back of his belt, well out of his way. He went outside and stood for a moment, blinking in the sunlight, and then he set off for Ylga's house. If she were still at home, he would bid her farewell; if not, she would know soon enough from others that he had been given a task which could not be delayed.

People were moving slowly through the streets, making their way toward the Assembly ground where the races and wrestling and archery contests would be held. Many greeted him; to the questions of his friends he answered only that his father was sending him on an errand, and agreed that it was too bad he would have to miss the games. Ylga's family lived on that side of the town—indeed, their garden wall bordered the Assembly field—and he found her still at home, sitting on the wall with her small brother and half a dozen other children, telling them a story. It was the tale of Budri, and as he came around the corner of the wall, he heard her saying,

"—and wherever the monster settled, everything died, the people, the plants, the grass, the earth itself. So when the news was brought to the council they were all frightened, and no one knew what to do."

"It was the kraken, wasn't it?" said one of the children.

"Of course it was, stupid," said Ylga's brother. "Go on about how nobody knew what to do except Budri."

Thorgeir leaned against the stones, looking at Ylga's serious face as she bent close to the children. Her voice, low and thrilling, had the power to keep him as attentive as they were.

"That's right," she said. "Budri Brightface said, 'I will go to the goddess and ask her for help.' "

She glanced up, and her eyes met Thorgeir's. He motioned to her to continue.

"Budri armed himself, and set out. He went to the land east of the sun and west of the moon, the land beyond the north wind where the ground is frozen night and day, and nothing grows. There is nothing but rock there, as red as blood. There, beside a lake of black ice, he found the Tree Illthorn which bears neither fruit nor leaf, and between two of its roots lay the Temple of Arveid. Budri went in and found a hall, a thousand paces long, and inside that another hall a hundred paces long, and inside that a little chamber, and there was the goddess Herself, the Golden Maiden with golden hair, and eyes as blue as the sky.

"Then Budri told her about the coming of the kraken, and begged that she would save her people. And Arveid opened a chest, and took out three magical gifts. There was the helmet, Dark-hood, and whoever wore it could not be harmed. There were the boots, Long-stride, and whoever wore them could go seven miles at a step. And there was the sword, Direful, and whoever struck with it had no need to strike again. 'Take these gifts,' said the goddess—"

Thorgeir, at that moment, saw his father in the distance,

across the Assembly ground, walking slowly with Ragn the Peacemaker, deep in conversation. The sight brought him back to his duty.

"I wish I had those boots," he said. "Forgive me, Ylga. I must talk to you. I am going away."

She said to the children, "Stay here. Wait for me," and jumped lightly down. She took Thorgeir's arm and led him around the corner of the wall.

"What is it?" she said. "Where are you going?"

"An errand for the council, something important."

Her face was solemn. "So we were right, when we saw Athils come running this morning. Something is happening. Can you tell me?"

"You will know soon enough, and so will everyone. The Tyrnings are making a settlement on Nimma's Field. I am being sent to—to watch the Pass of Voll."

"Is it war?"

"Not yet. I hope, not at all. But we will not meet tomorrow."

"When do you return?"

"In five days."

She was standing close to him, and she put her arms around his neck. "Oh," she murmured, "be careful."

He grew dizzy with her nearness, and kissed her. They were interrupted by the yells and cheers of the children, who had crept around the end of the wall to watch. He pulled away in embarrassment, but Ylga only laughed.

"Pests!" she said. "Go then, Thorgeir." And in a low, lov-

ing voice, she added, "Good be your going and swift your returning."

He touched her cheek, and left her. He walked to the
western edge of the town, where the old High Road began, a
wide track taken by trading parties and those coming and
going to the Midyear Market which was held alternately in
Velir and in Tyrgard. Its pale dusty ribbon stretched away for
forty miles to the Pass of Voll, over the mountains. Without a
backward glance, he began to run.

The nine miles to the hamlet of Brekka he covered easily,
pacing himself, going light and steadily. For the first couple of
miles stone walls edged the road, and beyond them was pas-
tureland in which little, shaggy, short-legged cattle grazed.
Then the walls ended and there was rank, weedy grass, dotted
with clumps of trees, thick and ancient, their rough trunks
stained with moss, their branches lively with new leaves.
They were called eika. At Brekka, which was no more than a
dozen houses surrounded by fenced meadows, fields of kala
beans coming into yellow flower, and the inevitable selva, he
left the road. The villagers were watching children dancing,
and some waved to him as he passed.

And now he began running in earnest. He crossed rolling
ground, like a sea swell, where there grew low, soft-stemmed
bushes covered with lavender blossoms that hummed with in-
sects. The sun was high but, at this time of year, not blazing;
nevertheless, the water soon streamed down his face. He
stopped and lay down for a three-minute rest. Under his

belt he had tucked the ends of two kerchiefs, and he tied one of them about his forehead to keep the sweat out of his eyes.

On the horizon, the purplish-blue line of the mountains rose higher. The rolling ground gave way to a long valley where corners and edges of rock thrust up, starred with the gray rings of old lichens. Hour after hour he ran, pausing for short rests, wringing out and changing the kerchiefs about his head, letting one hang free to dry from his belt while he wore the other. Now and then, he took the tiniest of sips from his water bottle, or held a scrap of hard, dried meat between his teeth to give himself something to clench on. The westering sun made him squint, but he ran on, coming up out of the valley into a wide tilted plain where the ground was hard and little grew save large clusters of tough, pale puffballs which gave beneath his feet, sometimes without bursting.

The plain rose more steeply and began to be covered with thorny trees among which some lithe animals grazed, bounding away at his approach and then stopping to look after him. They were covered with whorls of blue fur, and their heads, on slender necks, had perpetual expressions of alarm. They were new to him, but he could spare them no thought. Ahead, now, and running back on his right, towered the hogback of Blackfell Ridge, and on the left the trees gathered into the outliers of a vast forest, like a thunder cloud stretching across the land.

He threw himself flat, panting. Behind the loom of Blackfell the sky was orange, paling upward to yellow and then pale blue, with a few fleecy gray clouds all gilded on their undersides. Long draperies of rock fell steeply from the ridge which led away northward, rising at last in pale peaks which vanished in the darkling air. This was the range of Baldrock through which cut the Pass of Voll.

Thorgeir marked out his direction, looking wistfully at the forest which thinned out directly ahead of him to meet the lower slopes of Blackfell, over which he must go. It would be shorter through the wood, but his father had been very positive in his warning. He could see that he would have to run uphill over broken ground perhaps another ten miles until he reached a smooth, barren slope and there he could see, sharp against the burning sky, the great bulging knoll of which Frodi had spoken.

He stood up and tightened his belt. He clasped his hands before him and began to breathe deeply and slowly. His eyes were upon the land ahead, now deepening into dusk, and he could feel his body growing lighter and filling with air. His mind emptied of everything but the knoll in the distance. He was entranced, "breathborn." He began to run once more, staring straight before him at the sky over the slope, its color darkening moment by moment, and the first bright star hanging in it like a beckoning lamp.

Without knowing how he had come there, without remembering climbing or leaping, he stood gasping at the top of the knoll, some time later. The sky had lightened with the multitude of stars, and particularly the five brilliant ones called the Ale Horn, which on so clear a night cast a faint shadow about his feet. There were potholes scooped into the stone and thick moss growing in them. He lay down on the moss and slowly felt himself come to life again, his legs tingling, the throbbing in his chest and head subsiding. He had covered nearly half of the journey; tomorrow, with a longer day, he would be less pressed and he should be in Liskhavn before evening.

There was no camp to be made. He ate hard biscuit, dried meat and dried fruit, and drank sparingly. From the bottom of his pack he took a thin, light rectangle of waterproof cloth and wound himself in it. With his head on his pack and his sword beside it, he fell asleep at once.

The first light in the sky and the thin fluting of a rock lizard woke him. He knelt on the moss and gave thanks to Udi for another day, ate lightly, and shouldered his pack. He looked westward, but all the land ahead still lay in shadow, for the sun was not yet risen behind him, where Velir lay. Still, he fancied he could see a faint shining of water which must be Brine Lake.

He began the descent. On the other side the knoll dropped steeply in a series of slanting ledges, and it took him an hour to climb down. But below, the land was flat, at first thinly wooded, then more and more open, so that the running was easy and he had not to drive himself too hard. By noon, he was in a sea of grass, knee-high but soft and yielding, and grazed by herds of docile, long-bodied beasts whose fleecy, spotted coats brushed the ground. They had each a single long white horn in the forehead, beneath which were markings like raised eyebrows over their round eyes. As he passed, one after another their heads rose and they stared at him with drooling astonishment.

Boggy patches began to appear, and the ground was wetter. Guiding by the sun, he had been steering southwest and now he could in fact see the blink of water ahead. After a little while he came to a road. It was hardly more than a track, but it was clearly marked and had been reinforced with stone at the wettest places. It crossed his path, coming perhaps from some hamlet near the mountains, above where he had crossed, and going to the lake. Standing on it and looking west, so flat was the countryside that he could see far off the irregular line of rooftops outlined against the glimmer of the water; that must be Liskhavn. He girded himself for the last few miles.

The track he was on joined a wide, well-made road stretching north and south, and Thorgeir stopped and sat down to rest. This road, he guessed, was the Salt Track along which went the carts loaded with their precious cargo from the pans at Liskhavn, going to Tyrgard. Scarcely a mile away, to his left, the town stretched along the shore and he could see the glittering patches of drying salt and smell its brisk tang. He drank the last of his water and set out to walk there, so as not to arrive breathless, for the sake of honor.

All gray and white was the town of Liskhavn, its wooden houses weathered gray and saturated with crystals of brine from the air. Its fields were flourishing, for the salt air was good for growing, and around the neat gardens grew dark red and orange flowers with purple stems and leaves which made a pleasing contrast with the bleached wood. Thorgeir thought it a cheery place, not at all like a town of unbelievers.

He walked slowly, looking about with interest. An old woman was digging in the plot in front of her house, and he stopped and leaned on the fence.

"Health to you, mother," said he. "Can you tell me where to find the house of Hjal Broadbiter?"

She paused, looking at him suspiciously out of narrow, red-rimmed eyes, munching her lips. Then she said, "Who are you? Where do you come from?"

He had an uneasy feeling that he had said something wrong, but couldn't imagine what it was. Nor was he prepared for her questions, and said, in confusion, "From the mountains."

She came toward him, thin and hunched, holding her spade in both hands like a spear, and said, "From the mountains? There is nobody in the mountains except the devils and worshipers of devils. Who are you, eh, giving no proper greeting and dropping from the sky, eh? What mountains?"

"I—I'm sorry—" Thorgeir stammered.

"The Lord Udi sees your heart, young man," screeched the old woman. "He knows what lies you are hiding. You are one of *them*, aren't you, eh? Foul wicked heretics—drinkers of the blood of maidens! I know one when I see one."

Thorgeir backed away, bumping into someone who had

come up behind him. It was a stocky man with a wooden rake over one shoulder. He was grinning, showing yellow teeth in a red beard, and he held up a hand.

"Be calm, Skagga, be calm," he said. "Can't you see you are frightening the young man out of his wits?" And to Thorgeir, in a lower tone, he added, "Best come with me."

He led Thorgeir down the lane and around a corner, out of sight of the old woman. "We redheads must stick together," he said.

"Thank you," said Thorgeir. "I don't know what I said or did that started her off—"

"The sight of a stranger is sometimes enough," said the other. "She comes from Modru, that was under the mountain and is gone now. Her family was slain in the raid by strangers from over there," and he jerked his head to the east. Then, looking Thorgeir up and down, "You've come a long way. What was it you wanted?"

"To find Hjal Broadbiter."

"That is easy enough. Follow this lane straight along, and when you come to the end you will see a large house with a red painted door on your right. News from Tyrgard, from the council, I suppose?"

"Ah . . . not exactly," Thorgeir answered, incapable of a lie. "It's something—a message from my father. Thank you again for your help."

"Nothing."

The man raised a hand in salute, making an odd gesture,

his middle finger bent and crossed over his forefinger. Thorgeir smiled, turning away with a wave of his hand, and so did not see the other's eyebrows rise, nor the frown that settled on his face as he looked after him.

A woman answered Thorgeir's knock. Her shining gray hair hung straight to her shoulders, making her pale, rather severe face look sterner still. Her voice, however, was soft and agreeable.

"Come in, and welcome," she said. "Hjal is at work upon a poem and no one dares disturb him unless it is a matter of life or death. But—"

"Tell him," Thorgeir broke in, earnestly, "that it *is* a matter of life or death."

The woman eyed him for a moment, and then motioned him to enter. She led him through the great hall where a man and a woman were setting out mugs and platters on a long table. Thorgeir had forgotten how late it was, and a twinge of hunger went through him. The woman brought him through a passage lined with carved wooden panels, and stopped before a low, heavy door. She rapped with her knuckles.

"Go away," said a voice inside.

"It's important. A visitor. He says it's a matter of urgency."

There was no answer.

Thorgeir touched the woman's arm and motioned her to let him come to the door. With his lips close to it, he said, "Hjal, I am Thorgeir Frodi's-son."

A chair scraped; an instant later, the door was flung open. A man of middle height, whose shoulders filled the opening, regarded Thorgeir and then caught him by the arms.

"I would know you by your eyes if nothing else," he said. "Your father told me, 'One green, one blue, as if he couldn't choose between his mother and me.' "

He turned to the woman, who was staring. "You know who this is, Gerda?" She nodded. "Fetch some ale," he said. "Let us greet the guest properly."

He drew Thorgeir into the room. It was small, and seemed smaller with Hjal's bulk in it. He was a man made for joviality, with a large veined nose, bushy curling moustachios, twinkling blue eyes. He was not fat, but wide and solid and looked like one who sampled with delight everything that came to him on life's plate. He pushed Thorgeir into the armchair before a table littered with sheets of paper, reed pens, book-scrolls, and ink bottles. He himself sat on a low stool, hands on thighs, puffing a little from excitement.

"When did you leave your father?" he asked.

"Yesterday, a little past noon," said Thorgeir.

Hjal opened his eyes wide. "By Udi," he said, "that was a run. Now I know you are your father's son. Did you hear that, Gerda?" he said, as the woman came in with a pitcher and three mugs. "Near a hundred miles in less than thirty hours. By Tyr, I could not have done it at his age."

"Yes, you could," said Gerda, with a smile. She poured out ale, and handed a mug to Thorgeir.

Hjal took a mug, also, and said formally, "Welcome be the guest to hall and hearth. Rest beneath this roof as if it were your own."

"Health and thanks to you," replied Thorgeir, and drank. "You had no trouble finding me?"

"A little. I asked an old woman, but I must have said something wrong, because she flared out at me and accused me of—" He paused, not knowing how to say it. "She guessed where I came from, I think," he ended.

Hjal and Gerda exchanged a glance. "Ah," said Hjal. "Of course. A thin, bent old woman wearing a red stocking cap?"

"Yes. A man came along and helped me. He called her Skagga."

"Of course," Hjal repeated. "You did not greet her with the proper sign. It was how her husband and her daughters died." And he held up his hand, the middle finger bent and crossed over the forefinger.

Thorgeir remembered, then, how the redheaded man had saluted him. "What does it mean?"

"We often use it in greeting or farewell," said Hjal. "It is the rune *en*—" He drew it on the table with a finger: ᛉ . "It stands for the name Niala, which Arveid took for the first year when she came to earth as a mortal woman. And it stands, too, for the shears with which she cut off her golden hair, for we say that it fell below her feet when she was with Udi, but when she had to walk upon the earth she cut it short. The strangers—your people, unfortunately—who came to Skagga's village, greeted her without making that sign, and then drew their swords for the slaying. She was wounded, but escaped."

"I would you had never seen her," said Gerda. "It will mean trouble."

"Perhaps not," Hjal said. "Let us not bleed before we are stricken."

" 'Word moves, although mouth stands still,' " quoted Gerda, shaking her head.

Hjal emptied his mug and set it down on the floor. "You have not run so hard and so long simply to greet me, Thorgeir. Why have you come?"

Thorgeir could not keep from glancing at Gerda, but Hjal said, "She and I are one. Speak. I can see that it is important."

"It may mean war," said Thorgeir. "Some of your folk have settled on the high ground called Nimma's Field, not far from Esk. Word came to our council in Velir, and at least one councillor is urging us to fight. My father has done what he could to soothe matters, but he has had to summon the High Moot. They will assemble in Velir in three days more, and on the day after that they will meet. He thought you might not know of the settlement, nor your council how grave the matter might become."

"But I know," said Hjal, with a heavy sigh. "The proposal was made at the Jul-moot, before the year's end, and in spite of all I could do, and those who felt as I do, it was decided to establish the settlement as soon as the snows had melted."

"But do they not understand—?"

"They understand well. There are some new councillors since the last elections, hotheads who have found a following and have been planning this for a long time. Their scheme is clever. Either to draw the Vollings to the north to attack the settlement, in which case the main body of our folk will strike at Velir itself, or, if the Vollings do not move against the settlement, to seize Esk and its mines. If they hold the mines, they hold the upper hand."

Thorgeir listened, aghast. "Then," he said, "there is no hope of bargaining?"

"None. They say that they will put an end to the heretics once and for all. Those of the Vollings who are not slain will be converted to the true faith."

"The true faith," said Thorgeir, bitterly. "It is on both sides, and it means only manslaying."

Gerda and Hjal exchanged a glance. Gerda said, "It seems to me you do not think as others do."

Thorgeir replied, "Perhaps I will offend you if I say that I cannot hate those who think otherwise from me. When I was younger I shared a room with my brother, Athils. He and I agreed but little, and yet there was space enough for us both. Two men may cast at the same mark with different spears and still find it."

Hjal smiled. "You do not offend us. You are wiser than your years, and no doubt you have suffered for it. There may be one truth which is seen in different ways. Once, long ago, we all had the same religion. I have studied the matter. A hundred and twenty years ago came the Separation—the preaching of Bjarni Sword-tongue, who went into the wilderness of the north, to that place called the Meadow of Arveid, and who returned saying that he had seen the Holy Temple and had learned the truth, which was that Arveid had been sent by Udi, her Father, to live upon earth as a woman and save humankind. He it was, Bjarni Tyrna's-son, who divided us all. Maybe," he added, heavily, "it was the truth he found, but I think sometimes the truth can be more of a curse than a blessing."

"The wrong is not in the truth," said Gerda, "but in men's use of it."

They sat in silence for a time, and then Thorgeir said, "So there is nothing you can do."

Hjal shook his head. "Oh, no doubt there will be another High Moot in Tyrgard if the Vollings send a delegation to us. I will speak for peace and I can be sure of some others to back me, but not enough, I fear, to change the vote. It will only delay things. But at least, with what I have told you, your father can be alert. In that case, the bloodshed will be less and the war sooner over. It is the most we can hope for."

Thorgeir sat with his hands between his knees, feeling a great weight of oppression settle over him. The fatigue of his journey, which he would have thrown off had things been brighter, now filled his limbs so that he felt he would never move again.

He roused himself, to say, "I must return to my father."

"Not without a day of rest," Gerda said, firmly. She rose,

gathering up the mugs and pitcher. "For now, let us put these things out of our minds. Dinner will be ready soon, and before then you must cleanse yourself of the dust of your running. Orm will no doubt have some clothes that will fit you."

"She means my nephew, Orm Handskill," Hjal explained. "He lives with us, to learn the salt trade. Go, then, Thorgeir, and we will talk later, for I have much to ask you about Frodi."

Orm proved to be a dark, quiet youth, so reticent indeed that Thorgeir wondered how he would ever find words to buy and sell salt. He was much of a size with Thorgeir, perhaps a little longer in the arm, and he brought out a sober russet-colored tunic and trews. When Thorgeir had come from the steam room and the plunge and had pulled them on, buckling his own belt about the trews, Orm said, "That is well," and without another word led him to the hall.

Sixteen kemperymen, and laborers both men and women, sat down to dinner together below Hjal and Gerda, and nothing was stinted them of food and drink, plain fare but of the best quality. It seemed to Thorgeir a happy household.

He and Orm sat at the foot of the table, and busied themselves with eating. Thorgeir, in any case, was too hungry to mind the silence. But at last, he pushed away his plate and said, "Now I am alive again."

"I have heard how wonderful was your run," said Orm.

"So you *can* talk!" Thorgeir grinned.

Orm blushed, smiling in return. "I did not wish to disturb you. I thought you must be weary."

"You were right. I shall sleep tonight."

"It was a great feat."

Now it was Thorgeir's turn to redden. "No, no. In any case, it had to be done. Hjal is your uncle, is he? Where is your home?"

"In Vestastur, to the west of Tyrgard. It is different there, from here," he said, wistfully. "There are pleasant little valleys among the high hills, and the hills are crowned with old trees growing in circles. We used to say that the trolls planted them. They make good places to play, and when I was a child I used to play with my friends there, games of wars, of raiding the unbelievers."

He cocked a humorous eye at Thorgeir. "We called you Maggots."

"Ah," said Thorgeir, "and in our games we called you Stink-people."

Orm took up his mug and swished the ale about in it. "Well, I do not play such games any longer." He grinned. "You do not seem so very maggoty to me, but perhaps you hide it well. Some day perhaps I will take you to see Vestastur. But you must pretend—"

He broke off. There had come a loud knocking on the outer door of the house, clearly heard above the noise at the tables. A kemperyman rose, and at a nod from Hjal went to open the door. There came in two people, one the redheaded man who had helped Thorgeir, the other a woman with a grim, bony face, whose rough black cloak and black wooden staff proclaimed her to be a spaewife.

The spaefolk alone came and went between the Vollings and Tyrnings as they liked, safe from all harm. They were all of them a little mad but they had a useful gift. It happened sometimes, very rarely, that a child would be born who, instead of playing as other children did, sat alone much and drew pictures, and when these pictures were examined they were found to contain something relating to the future of those near to them, a gold coin, a heart, a bloody knife. Such a child would be apprenticed to a spaeman or spaewife, and when it was older sent to wander over the world until it found a place where it wished to live. Then, when anyone needed advice about some doubtful outcome, the spaer was called upon, who, putting himself or herself into a sleep, would draw a picture in which was hidden a foresight of what might come.

This woman strode up to Hjal and Gerda and stood before them without a greeting. However, the redhaired man beside her said, "Health to you and peace to the hall."

"And to you, Ketl. What brings you here at so late an hour?" said Hjal, stroking his beard. "And Skuld also. I do not remember having asked to see the future."

"But I have," said Ketl. "And it will come to you whether you ask or not."

"That is as may be," Hjal said. "What can be seen can be avoided, and then it is no longer the future. But I cannot have guests standing in my hall. Will you not sit and drink a cup?"

"No guest-cup will I drink until I have said my say," replied Ketl, with a stubborn thrust of his chin. "And it is this: people are saying that there is a maggot in your meat, and if it is not plucked out they will come and pluck it out for you."

Hjal's face grew red and he drew his brows together, groping at his belt for his dagger. "Have you come to beard me with such words in my own hall?" he said. "By the spear of Udi, I will thrust them down your throat."

But Gerda put a hand on his and stilled him. A faint smile was on her pale, severe face.

"I know that Ketl Ari's-son has never been an unfriend to this house," she said. "Nor can I think he comes as an enemy now. Let us hear what people they are who are saying such a thing, and also why you have brought Skuld with you, for she, at least, has no part in any quarrel."

Her soothing tone relaxed the tension, and Ketl nodded. "That is true, and I have come to try if things can be settled without bloodshed. A young man came to this house earlier—" He searched about, and his eyes met those of Thorgeir. "Before then, he had asked the way of old Skagga, whose suspicions were roused because he did not greet her properly. And also, because he said that he came from the mountains. 'Ill news travels fastest,' as they say, and it was not long before she had spread the word among her neighbors. Now they have met, and the talk is that they will come to see if there is indeed an unbeliever here, and if so to do him a mischief.

"I, myself, met the young man. I do not know whether he came for good or ill, but I saw that he did not know how to make the sign of the shears. When the news of what Skagga was doing reached me, I went to try if I could smooth their feathers. It was agreed that I should ask advice of Skuld, and that I have done."

He had a piece of paper tucked under his belt, and he drew it forth, unfolded it, and laid it on the table before Hjal and Gerda. They bent forward, their heads together, to study it.

Gerda said, "A sword flying in the air between two men. What does it mean?"

Skuld spoke for the first time, in a dry, husky voice.

> *Sad is that token   and ill the seeing;*
> *Strife between brothers   the sword portends.*

With that, she pulled her cloak more closely about her, turned, and went out of the hall.

Then Hjal said, thoughtfully, "I ask your pardon, Ketl, for I see you came as a peacemaker, and your intention was good. Yet, as you know, I am not one who gives much thought to spaefolk or their warnings."

"But this warning," said Ketl, "is clear, and even if I had not brought Skuld with me to prove it, you could have seen it for yourself."

"What would you have me do?"

"Send the youth away," Ketl replied, promptly. "At once."

Hjal said, with a frown, "He has journeyed hard, a long way, and he is wearied. Besides, he came on an errand of friendship."

"I do not ask why he came, although others may. I say only that it is better one should suffer than that neighbors should fall out."

Hjal shook his head. "I have given him a welcome to hearth and hall. Shall it be said that the Tyrnings break the guest-oath? And because of the croaking of a poor crazy old woman like Skagga? I would sooner cut off my hand."

Before any more could be said, Thorgeir rose and stepped forward.

"May I speak?" he asked, and without waiting for an answer, went on, stammering a little in his earnestness. "I would be shamed forever if it were said of me that I brought danger to this house. I will go tonight."

Hjal looked at him with troubled eyes. "I will not hear of it."

"You have no choice but hear of it," said Thorgeir, firmly. "It is not you I must face, but my father. What do you think he would say to me?"

Hjal was silent.

Thorgeir turned to Ketl. "I thank you for your warning. Will you believe me if I tell you that although my faith is different from yours, I bear you no enmity? I cannot tell you why I came here, but I swear to you that it was not to do hurt to you or your neighbors."

Ketl looked at Thorgeir with approval on his blunt, flat face. "I believe you," he said. "You have honor, and you are prudent, as well."

"We redheads must stick together," said Thorgeir, trying to smile.

Gerda's cool voice cut in. "Thorgeir, I cannot force you to act against your will. But we, too, have our honor. As Hjal has said, the guest-oath is sacred. It is stronger even than the fears of Skagga. Go back to the others, Ketl, and say that our guest will rest himself beneath this roof tonight, and that in the morning he will go, and not before. And if they will not abide by this and leave him scatheless, tell them that I, Gerda Ragna's-daughter, whom men call Gerda Fairspeech, will bring them to suit at the next council as breakers of custom, and that I and mine will be at feud with them all forever, though the whole world be riven into splinters for it!"

Her voice had risen and it rang like a trumpet. When she was done there came a thunder of fists pounding on the tables in approval. Thorgeir felt his heart lift, and thought to himself that this was a woman he could love as he had loved his mother.

Ketl bowed his head. "I will tell them," he said. "And you have my promise that I will do all in my power to make them obey."

"Whatever happens," said Hjal, "I will not forget that you have stood friend to us in this matter."

Ketl turned away, but stopped beside Thorgeir. "Have

you a weapon?" he said, in a low voice, and before Thorgeir could reply he unbuckled his sword belt and thrust it into Thorgeir's hands.

"I cannot—" Thorgeir began, but Ketl was already half-way to the door and paid no further heed to him.

III

THE SHORT WAY HOME

IN THE morning when he awoke, Thorgeir lay for a few moments looking out through the open sliding doors of the bed-closet at the unfamiliar room, remembering the events of the night before. The sword Ketl had given him hung from one of the pegs on the wall beside his clothes, and at last he got out of bed and went to look more closely at it. The belt and scabbard were of bullock's hide, plain and showing the signs of long wear, but the buckle was of gold cast in the form of a pair of shears. The sword blade was three spans long, somewhat longer than his own, and of fine gray steel, perfectly balanced and so keen he could have shaved with it. The hilt, of fluted hardwood, had a pommel of some polished, dark red stone. Thorgeir shook his head; it was a gift worthy of a Speaker, and he could not understand why Ketl had given it to him. In the end, he put it down to the man's friendship for Hjal and Gerda. He was too modest and too innocent to gauge the effect his own courage, his sense of honor, had on others.

He dressed himself in his old clothes, which had been washed and dried for him, tied up his knapsack, and buckled on the new sword. His own belt and sword, and Orm's clothing, he carried out to the hall. There he found Hjal and Gerda alone at the table, waiting for him.

Gerda rose, cut bread for him, and poured out a beaker of milk. Hjal said, "Have you slept well?"

"Very well. I hope I haven't angered you by my decision."

Hjal smiled sadly. "We are as proud of you as your father will be. But I wish matters were otherwise. It galls me to give way to these narrow-minded fools."

"Sit down and eat," said Gerda. "You will need strength. I see you wear Ketl's gift. You have left a well-wisher behind you."

"He did not even wait to be thanked," Thorgeir said.

"It is his way," said Hjal.

"I am too much in his debt," Thorgeir sighed. He spread salt butter on a slice of bread, and began to eat.

"Do not think so. He is open-handed and generous, and cares nothing for possessions. He took a liking to you and gave you the first thing that came to hand."

Thorgeir finished his meal, while Gerda packed his knapsack with fresh provisions and refilled his water bottle. He rose to go, beginning, "Where is—" but at that moment, Orm came in.

"Ah, I was about to ask for you," said Thorgeir. "Here are your clothes. I hope some day to lend you mine. And I thought, perhaps—perhaps you would have these as keepsakes."

He held out his belt and sword. Orm hesitated. Thorgeir said, grinning, "Go on. I have no further need of them and if you will not take them, I will only have to throw them away."

Orm laughed, and said, "Since you now wear the sword of a Stink-person, I can wear that of a Maggot. Let us hope we will have no need to draw them today." And seeing Thorgeir's puzzled look, he added, "I am coming with you, at least as far as the foothills of Blackfell."

"What?"

"My uncle and aunt have no objection. They agree with me that it would be as well for you to have a friend with you."

Thorgeir said nothing, but gripped Orm so tightly by the hand that he winced. But Hjal said, " 'Bare is back without brother behind it.' Go, then, and swiftly, for the sun has risen."

And indeed, a long shaft of golden light spilled through the small windows and brightened the hall.

Orm buckled on the sword, and took up a long staff which leaned against the wall, near the door. It was made of black wood, footed with iron, and at its head was an iron fork of two blunt prongs, five or six inches long. Hjal and Gerda embraced Thorgeir, and the two young men went out into the lane. Orm led the way, between two small houses and over a stile which led to a little raised path between the selva fields. The long rows of fresh, young, green leaves lay in their ribbons of shining water, stretching away on either hand, and they looked so familiar and homelike that they gave Thorgeir a pang.

He said, "So all the water hereabouts is not salt?"

"No. The water lies everywhere only a little way below the surface, and coming up through the earth grows sweet. They have no need of reservoirs, as we do in Vestastur."

The path led eastward, and with the sun in their eyes they began to trot. The fields spread for nearly a mile on that side of the town, ending at higher but still level ground, covered with springy turf.

"Now," said Orm, "I have brought you this way because it is shorter than the way you came. This is good running ground, so let us make use of it."

Side by side, they set off at a long, striding lope, breathing easily and deeply. They had not gone more than half a mile, when Orm said, "We have guests."

Ahead, and to their left, some distance off but easy to see in that flat land, three figures were running, making a long slant to cut them off.

"Shall we go faster?" said Orm. "It may be we can outrun them."

Thorgeir stopped. "I do not like to have them at my back," said he. "I had rather meet them face to face and hear what they have to say."

"I, too, like to hear good conversation," said Orm, cheerfully.

They stood and waited, Thorgeir hitching his sword hilt around closer to hand, and Orm leaning on his staff. The three figures paused, moved together as if talking, and then began trotting toward them. Close by, they stopped, spreading a little apart. One was burly and blond, with an extravagant moustache, one crafty-looking and pimply, the third a tall, likely youth with an aquiline nose and a reckless, swaggering air; he reminded Thorgeir of his brother, Athils. He wore a sword, the others carried long-handled axes.

The sword wearer stepped forward and said to Orm, "This is not your quarrel. Go home."

"Well, well," said Orm. "I thought you were a brave man, Oli, but I see you will not fight unless the odds are three to one."

"I will make sure of you, at any rate," said Oli, and with a rasp of metal whipped out his sword. In the same movement, it seemed, so swift was his hand, he struck a great downward blow at Orm's head.

What followed happened almost too fast to be seen. Orm had been standing lazily, with his staff in both hands. He brought it up and caught the blade in the iron fork; he twisted the staff, and the blade sailed high in the air.

Thorgeir caught his breath. It was exactly as Gerda had described the picture drawn by the spaewife—two men and a sword flying up between them. The next instant, the tall man lay on his back, knocked senseless by a blow from the iron-shod foot of the staff.

The blond one sprang forward, swinging his axe. Thorgeir's sword was out, and he leaped to meet the other, shouting to draw his attention. The axe whistled through the air, cleaving the spot where Thorgeir's head would have been had he not dropped into a crouch, anticipating the blow. He straightened before the blond man could recover, lunged up-ward, and stabbed him through arm and shoulder.

As the blond man staggered back, clutching at his wound, Thorgeir spun round to help Orm, but Orm needed no help. Laughing, he parried the blows of the third man's axe, turning them aside with the iron fork. He held the man off with the butt until Thorgeir had joined him.

"Drop your axe," said Thorgeir, harshly, "and be glad you come out of this no worse. Go, help your friend tie up his wound."

"Stinking heretic," said the pimply man. Nevertheless, he let fall his weapon.

Orm picked up both axes. The sword had fallen point first and was sticking in the turf. Orm plucked it out. The youth, Oli, still lay where he had fallen and Orm looked doubtfully at him.

"He is not dead," said Thorgeir. "I see his chest rise and fall. You there," he said, to the pimply man, "get him up on your shoulders. Now, be off."

"You foul Maggot," said the blond man. "Don't think you will escape. We are not the only ones."

Thorgeir watched as they staggered away, the pimply one with the limp body of his friend over his shoulder, the blond one holding the bloody bandage that covered his wound.

Then he said, looking at Orm with admiration, "Never have I seen such a thing—a man with a stick overcoming a swordsman!"

Orm replied, "I learned that art because one cannot escape fighting, but I do not wish to take any man's life."

"Nor I," said Thorgeir, more drawn to Orm than ever. "Rightly are you called Handskill. I will come and be your pupil some day. But for now, perhaps it would be wiser for us to part. You heard what he said. There must be others of them following."

"Or ahead of us, hoping to waylay us. I would guess them to be waiting along the Modru road—the road you came on from the mountains."

"Then go back, Orm. That one spoke rightly, it is not your quarrel."

"I have made it my quarrel," Orm said. He cast away the two axes and the sword. "Let us go. We will bear southward, swinging away from the line of the road, before we turn east again."

They began to run, with no further speech.

The turf thinned and became patchy; the ground was harder and studded with clumps of slender white trees with broad fronds which rattled in the wind. From their tops, frilled lizards called in clear, sweet voices. Stony ridges, shelves of pebbly earth that fell away into shallow dales, made the running harder. They came up out of one such long gully and saw, far ahead, a dark irregular line stretching all across the horizon, and off to the left the pale, misty-blue mass of the mountains. The sun was nooning, and they sat down to rest and eat.

"That is the forest ahead," said Orm. "We can be nearly there by nightfall."

Thorgeir closed his eyes, summoning up the map on the table in the council hall.

"I am ahead of time," he said, "since I did not spend this day resting in Liskhavn. On the other hand, I am wearier than when I started from Velir." He shaded his eyes, looking east and then northeast. "Perhaps," he mused, "I could try going through the wood, after all. It will save me a long run north to Blackfell."

"I will keep you company until tonight," said Orm. "You can decide then."

Evening found them on the lip of a slope, below which lay a deep, wide valley some three miles or more across. On its further edge marched mighty trees bearing on their upraised limbs huge crowns of leaves, so dark a green as to be almost black. Clouds had come piling out of the west and the setting sun had been covered, so that the wood looked ominous.

"We will camp here," said Thorgeir.

They were both tired, and spoke little. After a scanty dinner, they rolled up in their blankets in the shelter of some low bushes, and fell asleep almost at once. During the night, a driving, drizzling rain in their faces woke them, but their sleeping-cloths had been well rubbed with the fat of tree-mice and kept off the wet. They covered their heads and went back to sleep.

The drizzle ended before morning, as usual at this time of year when there was little rain. They got up cold and ate a cold breakfast, but like warriors ignored their discomfort. They shouldered their packs and turned to look at each other.

Thorgeir said, "I do not know whether we shall ever meet again, but—if you would—I will swear brotherhood with you."

For answer, Orm drew the sword Thorgeir had given him and unhesitatingly made a small cut in his forearm. Thorgeir did the same. They held their arms together and let their blood mingle.

Then Orm said, "I will show you a wonder."

He untied the strings of his shirt and opened it. Around his neck was a thin gold chain, from which hung a circular flat pendant. Thorgeir stooped to look at it. It was not much bigger than the top joint of his thumb, and made of polished steel with an oddly frosty surface. In its center was a disk of shining gray, and set in one side was a small blue stone.

"This," said Orm, with awe in his voice, "came back with Bjarni Tyrna's-son from the Temple of Arveid, more than a hundred years ago. There are a pair of them, and they were given long ago by the great-grandson of Bjarni to his wife, Ogna Goldhead, who was the great-great-grandmother of my uncle, Hjal Broadbiter. My uncle gave this one to me, early this morning, when I told him that I hoped you would have me for a friend. And the other—"

"Yes?"

"Your father has it. You must tell him that Hjal asks him to give it to you."

Thorgeir touched the pendant gingerly. "It is very old, very strange. I will ask him, but perhaps—"

"You do not understand. It is how my uncle and your father were able to meet each other. Have you never wondered how they could arrange to do so? For Hjal told me that they have met twice together in the past twenty-five years."

Thorgeir's mouth fell open.

"It is so," Orm said. "Listen. When this blue stone is pressed, the gray disk in the other amulet will glow with a light of its own. And also, if the blue stone in the other amulet is pressed, this one will glow. The glow lasts until the blue stone is pressed once more. Thus, whoever wears an amulet can signal to the other wearer even if they are half the world apart. Let us set a meeting place, and then, if ever one of us is in need or wishes to see his friend, we can send the signal."

"It is indeed a great wonder," said Thorgeir. "The magic of Arveid! It is like something from the saga of Budri. Perhaps that tale, too, is true."

"When you tell your father that Hjal has given me this, and that we are blood brothers, he will surely give you his amulet," said Orm. "Where shall we meet, then, at need?"

Thorgeir crouched, and picking up a sharp-pointed stone, drew a map in the dirt. "North of here, where the forest ends and Blackfell Ridge begins, if you climb up on the skirts of the mountain there is a great knoll of rock with many large holes and pockets of moss at the top and a steep cliff rising above it."

"Good," said Orm. "And now, farewell."

They clasped hands, and Thorgeir said, "Will they not try to take revenge on you for helping me?"

"I think not. They are cowards and will fear Hjal and Gerda. Nor will Oli wish me to tell everyone how he was worsted. I think they will let the matter drop."

Thorgeir turned away and began the descent into the valley. Glancing over his shoulder, he saw Orm leaning on his staff, watching him; when next he looked, the skyline was empty.

It seemed clear to him that the forest must be broader here than it was near the mountains, for the distance was shorter from Liskhavn: they had made the journey easily in a day, even with the interruption of a fight and their swing southward. He would have to strike northeast across the wood so as to lose no time. He could not run fast, for although there was little undergrowth, the woods were dense. But if he trotted steadily he could, he thought, do it in a day.

At first, all went well enough. The trees were mostly of two sorts, those huge, tall ones with heavy, dark leaves, called embla, and smooth-trunked more graceful ones, aska, with fluttering yellow leaves, like coins, in drooping strands. They grew far enough apart so that he could make his way between them, and the ground was covered with moss and with a short, fat-bladed juicy grass. As the sun rose, it struck down between the leaves, dappling the trunks and the earth with dancing golden spots and guiding him. Tree-mice sailed chittering from branch to branch, and now and again some small animal darted away too quickly to be seen as more than a blur. He kept a sharp lookout for those deadly beasts called ovinur, but saw no trace of them, and indeed they were seldom found in woods where the aska and embla grew thickly.

After a while, however, another kind of tree, unfamiliar to Thorgeir, began to appear. It was slender, with a black trunk and crimson five-pointed leaves which bloodied the daylight. It had many branches, interlacing and tangled, from which hung long brown pods, so that he was reminded of some beamed, dark kitchen with smoked sausages hanging from the ceiling. These trees were closer together, and the moss beneath them was damp and slippery, and from it grew tough toadstools which broke against his legs, covering them with an evil-smelling slime. He had to slow his trot, and at last dropped into a walk.

Then he came upon something which made the hair prickle on his neck. He emerged into a clearing where he thought, at first, that woodmen had been at work cutting timber. With a shock, he realized that something else had been at work, something unimaginably big which had smashed down the trees as if they had been reeds, and had stripped them of their leaves. Splintered stumps were everywhere, and broken branches, and tree trunks trampled into mud. Two trails met at the spot, wide enough for wagons to be pulled along them, one of trees broken down with their crowns pointing toward the clearing, the other leading away.

He hesitated for a long time there, listening, peering in every direction. Whatever had done this was so vast that it could stamp him out of life like a worm. The trail leading away was going roughly in the direction he had to go, but he thought, in the end, that he had better not take the chance of meeting whatever it was. From the clearing, he could see that the sun was westering and he headed away from it and from the two trails, slipping as softly as he could between the trees.

An hour later, perhaps, he came to a gully. It was hardly more than a crack where some long-ago earthquake had split the ground, but it was too wide to jump across and its wall, on Thorgeir's side, too sheer to climb down. It crossed his path and he had to turn northward. On and on he went, and the crack only widened, young saplings reaching from its depths, and the glint of a stream appearing. He began to worry, for he saw no way out of the forest, and the light, already dimmed from so many of the red-leaved trees, was fading still more as the sun sank.

Then the high bank of the gully began to drop away and the gully itself widened. The pale gray boles of askas appeared and the black trees thinned. He felt more lighthearted. Some while later, however, he was beginning to worry. Twilight had gathered about him and still there was no end to the forest. He sat down with his back against a smooth trunk, wiped his legs as best he could with leaves, and opened his pack. Before he had finished eating, darkness had come, more rapidly than in the open. He lay down, rolling himself in his sleeping-cloth, and tried to put out of his mind the disturbing thought that he was lost.

He awoke in the pitchy dark with the feeling that he was not alone. He lay utterly still, and above the surge of blood in his ears, he heard a faint crack as of something shifting its weight. There was some presence nearby, hardly more than a sense of warmth, of breathing, of the loom of a great body.

He dared not move. He was lying between the spreading roots of an aska and it might be that he was unobserved, while if he moved it was possible that the thing could see in the dark and would then be aware of him. But also, it might be that it had already seen him and was preparing for a spring. His sword was beside his head, and with infinite slowness he moved his hand to clasp the hilt.

Something touched his forehead. It was as light and soft as a blade of grass blown against him by a puff of wind. He stiffened, and in the next instant he would have been on his feet, sword drawn, except that there came into his mind an overwhelming calmness. His muscles loosened, his body relaxed, and he began to breathe again.

He still held the hilt of his sword. The touch on his forehead grew firmer, like the pressing of a finger, and the sense of peace strengthened. He let go the sword and sat up.

A clear image formed before his eyes, small and bright.

He saw himself sitting beneath the tree. Before him was a creature so huge that standing erect his head would have come no higher than its knee. It sat back upon its haunches, its great pale belly bulging and hairless, its upper body covered with a soft, dark brown pelt barred with black. Its forelegs were longer than the hind ones and ended in blunt-nailed paws like stumpy human hands. Its large, round head was fixed on a short neck, and at the sight of its face he lost whatever lingering fear he might have felt, for there was something at once comical and solemn about it. It had a short, thick snout that drooped over its pendulous lower lip, and beneath that snout it seemed to smile, while its small, wide-set eyes twinkled; they reminded him, all at once, of Hjal's eyes. Its forehead was high and bony, and from behind each platterlike ear grew a cluster of long and slender tentacles, like coarse hairs, that stirred, some of them rising and falling from time to time. One of these tentacles, he saw, was stretched forward to touch his forehead.

He said, aloud, "Who are you?" not conscious that he had said "who" instead of "what."

The image faded and he was in the dark once more, with only that warm, light touch on his brow. Then, although he heard nothing, words formed in his mind as if he himself were thinking them.

"I am Ylvan."

Mingled with the wonder in Thorgeir's mind was an obscure satisfaction that his father had only seen one from a distance.

He said, "What do you want of me?"

"*Of* you?" Could a voice without substance sound puzzled? "I want *to* you. To warn you. There is danger coming."

"Danger?" Thorgeir tensed, but again the feeling of calm flooded his mind.

"Not so soon," said the ylvan's thought. "Far away." It seemed to mean *far away* in time as well as distance. "You must warn your others, so that they may escape."

"What is the danger?"

"The danger?" The tentacle was removed and he felt nothing for a while, as if the beast were pondering. Then it touched him again. "You call it the kraken. It is coming."

It struck Thorgeir that he was dreaming. The voice speaking silently inside his head was like a voice heard in a dream. And to hear that the kraken was coming—that was utterly dreamlike. Was it to be believed that a creature from an ancient saga would appear out of the sky? Or that he himself was sitting in the dark talking to an ylvan inside his own head. He began to laugh. But he did not wake.

He fell silent, and the ylvan said, "I do not understand. You think that I am not here and that I do not say what I say. How can that be?"

"It is all too strange," said Thorgeir. Cautiously, he got to his feet. "Let me touch you."

He was not stopped. He moved forward, groping, and his hand felt warm fur and smooth, massive muscle beneath it. He let out a sigh and sat down again, for his legs were suddenly weak.

He said, "The kraken—how do you know it is coming?"

"My others have told me. We can speak to each other— but you cannot speak so to your others, for you have not these." And into Thorgeir's mind flashed an image of the great round head of the ylvan with the bunches of tentacles erect behind its ears, like bushes growing up around a rock. The image faded, and the silent voice went on, "There are not many of us and each of us needs much food, so we live far apart only coming together for mating and the care of our young. Thus we speak with these, summoning our mates and hearing each other's talk."

There was something so unearthly and yet so touching in the thought of the huge, lonely beast calling to its kind in silence across the forests that Thorgeir shivered and felt a pang of something deeper than pity.

"What is the kraken?" he asked. "What does it look like?"

"I will show you."

A jumble of white, pale blue, pale green formed in Thorgeir's mind, and at first he could make nothing of it. Then he saw that he was looking across a waste of ice and water beneath an empty sky, green water with jagged pinnacles of ice surrounding it so that the water lay in a bowl of a size he could not guess. Something lay upon the water, at first a glittering jelly the color of sky and water; it darkened and coagulated and as it did so, the water dwindled and sank. The jelly-like mass grew smaller and firmer, lost its translucence and was contained within a kind of skin, black, so it seemed, but showing an iridescence in the sunlight. It was thick and humped in the center, thinner all around its edges. The water was almost gone and the thing lay in a swamp crisped around its shores with ice.

And then it rose. Its thin edges flapped like monstrous wings, and it soared above the swamp, dropping water and a cloud of dark particles. It began to fly, skimming the ground at first, then rising higher. Beneath it, trees and grass appeared, and then for the first time Thorgeir could see how immense it was. Its shadow fell across the trees like a cloud. It sank upon them and lay for a while, and when it rose again there remained only stark, bare poles and stumps, and where the grass had been all was blackened and blighted as if from fire.

The picture vanished, and the ylvan said, "That is the kraken. It leaves desolation wherever it goes. It will take long to come here, but when it comes everything will die. I will flee before it, and so will all my others, and all those we can warn. So must you and your others."

And suddenly, it was real. Thorgeir thought of the selva, of all the labor of planting, cultivating and irrigating, and saw that ominous, flapping thing descend upon the fields. Even if the folk escaped, they would starve.

"I must go," he said. "But I cannot run in the dark. And I do not know where I am."

The ylvan said, "Show me in your head where it is you would go."

Thorgeir found that it was far from easy to make a picture in his mind and hold it there, but he did his best. He tried to

see the forest spreading out between Tyrningsland and Vollingsland, growing narrower in the north upon the slopes of
Blackfell. He moved his mind's eye as if flying above it, eastward, into the lands through which he had run, coming at last
to Brekka, and then his concentration failed.

"I see it," said the ylvan. "I cannot go there, but I can at
least take you part of the way. You are not so very far from the
edge of this wood. I will take you there, and then most of the
way toward that mountain you know."

"But how?"

"On my shoulders. Climb up. I will help you."

Thorgeir felt a little dubious at this, but he could think of
no good excuse. He scrabbled about in the dark until he found
his belongings. He folded his sleeping-cloth and stowed it
away, fastened on his sword-belt, thrust his arms through the
straps of his pack. Then he turned, to feel the touch of the ylvan's tentacle again.

In his mind, he saw the beast stooping and bending a
foreleg on which he could climb. He reached out, felt fur and
the leg beneath his foot. The breath of the ylvan was warm
and bittersweet, like new-cut grass; its fur had the winey scent
of leaves in autumn. He climbed up and straddled its short
neck, holding on by the bases of the tentacles on either side.
They were unexpectedly rough and ridged, like twigs.

"Hold on," said the silent voice. "Put your head down
close to mine, and have no fear."

It removed its tentacle from his forehead, so that Thorgeir

could neither hear nor see it, but only clutch desperately with hands and knees as it set off. It moved with great speed, with a kind of flowing motion, rocking only slightly for all its bulk. Thorgeir expected at any moment that they would collide with a tree—remembering those splintered paths he had seen—but the ylvan avoided touching anything, and except for the occasional swish of a low bough, from which the mound of the creature's head protected him, he would not have guessed they were in the wood.

Then, all at once, the darkness about them lightened and they were under the stars. The ylvan rushed on. Turning his head, Thorgeir saw the heavy shadow of the wood on the left and knew that his mount was going north. Even sheltered as he was, the wind of its passage whipped about him and he pressed his cheek closer to its head. He found that for all the strangeness of his position, his eyes kept closing.

The ylvan stopped. It knelt, and Thorgeir climbed stiffly down. He saw it, then, in the starlight, a towering bulk, far more impressive than it had shown in the tiny picture in his mind, the domelike head bent down to him, the great face at once tranquil, humorous and wiser than anything human.

One of the tentacles touched him briefly, and he heard, in silence, "Farewell." It left him, its brown back vanishing at once among the shadows of the trees. He fumbled out his sleeping-cloth and, just where he was, lay down and was asleep.

IV

THE HIGH MOOT

THE house of Frodi Heavyhand stood a little apart from its neighbors on that side of Velir nearest the selva fields. Its center, and oldest part, was built of logs, and two wings of smoothed boards had been added. On the end of one of these, a second story consisting of one small room had been erected, reached by an outside stair, and this was where Frodi retired to be private whenever he would. He had windows that looked over the roof of the house toward the town, and in the other direction toward a little copse of silver-trunked trees called byorkas. There was a small table, two or three rough stools, a shelf of book-scrolls, and a large armchair with pillows stuffed with sweet-smelling herbs. On the wall hung an old sword without a scabbard, its plain wooden hilt well polished, its blade oiled; it was the sword Frodi's father, Thorkil, had borne in his last battle when he was very old. He had thrown away the sheath and gone berserk into the fight, looking for death.

Here, now, sat Frodi, with Thorgeir on a stool before him,

the late afternoon sun lighting up the wooden walls and casting a red glance from the iron pommel of the old sword. A tiny frilled lizard flew down upon the windowsill, shook its thin wings, trilled a note and flew off again.

Frodi watched it from the chair. Then he said, heavily, "There is no hope, then? He can do nothing?"

Thorgeir said, "He will do what he can, but he fears it will be useless. He said, as I told you, that there are new council members who are determined on battle."

"I fear I will be able to do little here. Jodrunn herself has said that the more she thinks of it, the more she feels the danger of the Tyrnings lying above Nimma's Field. And Ragn the Peacemaker has told me that although he will vote for negotiation, he feels we should not be unprepared for war. Worst of all, your brother has declared himself on the side of Svip Leaper, and has spoken openly of what has happened although he knows that with the town and village councillors gathering here for the Moot, he should be silent until we meet."

"That is thoughtless," said Thorgeir. "He is too mad bent on winning fame. When is the Moot to be?"

"Tomorrow morning." Frodi combed his beard with his fingers, and sighed. "Well," he said, "you have done well, and more than well. Now tell me, how did Hjal look? What is his wife, Gerda, like? How did they receive you?" For Thorgeir, who had arrived in Velir not a quarter of an hour before and had gone at once to his father, had told him only of Hjal's reply to the message, but so far nothing else.

"He is noble, and Gerda is a woman second only to my mother," Thorgeir said. "They received me with as much love as if I had been their son. But now I must tell you everything that happened, for there is something very strange to be said. Only, first, give me a little water, for I am very weary."

"I am a fool," said Frodi, starting to his feet. He had a tall pitcher and a cup on the table, and poured out water for his son, mixing with it a little strong spirit made from aldin-fruit. As Thorgeir drank, Frodi stood beside him with a hand on his shoulder. Then he said, "Tell on."

So Thorgeir told him how he had met that woman, Skagga, and how Ketl Ari's-son had come into the hall to warn them of the hatred of some of the townspeople, and of Gerda's decision that Thorgeir should rest there for the night.

"And this man, Ketl, gave you his sword?" said Frodi. "I could be a friend to such a one. Let me see it."

Thorgeir undid the belt and handed it over. Frodi examined it and said, "The buckle is a pair of shears. I remember something about shears in their religion. They say Arveid cut off her hair to become human. By Udi's eye, it is a rich gift." He handed back belt and weapon. "Go on, for I see there is more to tell."

Thorgeir continued with the story of Orm's friendship, of their fight with the three men the next morning, of their run to the forest and of their parting.

"Yes," Frodi said, with a smile, "he was right. I will give you the twin to his amulet. And Hjal was right to give it away."

He opened his shirt, and removed from about his thick neck a chain on which hung a pendant like that one Orm had shown Thorgeir, of frosted steel, set with a disk of gray and a small blue stone. He handed it to Thorgeir.

"Hjal and I will have no further use for them," he said, "for I feel in my bones we shall not meet again."

Thorgeir slipped it over his head. It was warm from his father's chest, and he fancied it felt heavy with the weight of age.

"So you went through the forest?" Frodi said. "It was lucky you were not lost."

"I was lost," Thorgeir replied. "Now I must tell you what I still do not understand, something that may have been a dream, but if not—"

He paused, remembering above all else the sweet breath of the ylvan in his face. It had been no dream. He took a breath and told Frodi all the rest of the tale.

Frodi sat for a long time in silence, his chin propped on his hand, looking at the floor. At length, he said, "It is hard to believe. As you say, it may have been a dream."

"Did I dream I found my way by night through the wood, all the way to the foot of Blackfell? I woke late this morning, and it is from there that I have run all this day."

"But the kraken—! And to learn of it from an ylvan! How am I—how is anyone—to believe such a thing?"

He rose and walked to the window, and stood looking out over the rooftops. Then, without turning, he said, "If I were to bring this story to the Moot, do you know what they would say? They would say that I was cunning beyond measure, to try to get my own way by throwing a fairy tale in their faces to blind them."

"Who would say such a thing?" cried Thorgeir. "What I have told you is the truth."

"Svip would say so, and many would think him right." He thrust his chin out at his son. "What proof have you?"

Thorgeir could not answer.

After a time, Frodi said, "And if it *is* true, what difference will it make? The image the ylvan gave you was of something too big for us to oppose. Something big enough to swallow up trees!"

"From what I saw, I believe that it sucks all the water out of things," said Thorgeir. "Out of trees, grass, and all living things, for even the ylvan feared it."

"Yes, and it would destroy the selva. For you know that unless the selva has ample water from now until the time of its gathering, it withers and dies. If we ran away from that thing—the kraken, if we can believe it is that—how could we live? Can we keep all our folk alive by hunting small game in the forest?"

Frodi struck his hands together. "It is hopeless. One way or the other, whether the kraken comes or the Tyrnings fall upon us, it is the last fight, the end of things." His face was like stone. "It will be as it was foretold, Ragnarok, the Death of Udi and the unmaking of the world."

Thorgeir shrank back, childhood fears sweeping over him, memories of old tales, nightmares born of ancient sagas told him when he was young, the story of the Wolf that ate the sun, the snares of Surtr who was the enemy of God, the last great battle called Ragnarok which ended all things.

Frodi's expression softened as he looked at his son. "Do not think of it," he said. "Let me consider what is to be done. I will talk with Ragn, who is the wisest of us all. Meantime, go and refresh yourself, and sleep. I cannot say more than that all you have done has given me cause for pride in you."

Thorgeir rose, and for the first time the full weight of his weariness fell upon him. It was more than fatigue; he had born with him the dreadful news that nothing could be done to stop the coming of war, and beyond that the strange encounter with the ylvan and its fantastic tidings. He felt as though his legs had turned to water, and he faltered as he left the room.

He closed the door behind him, and there was Athils, several steps below the landing on the outer stair. For an instant, Thorgeir, in his confusion of mind, thought that his brother was going down, but then Athils came up and with what seemed an effort, smiled at him.

"So you are back—from the Pass of Voll," said Athils.

Thorgeir was too tired to mark the slight hesitation. "I am back," he said.

"Is all well?"

"Yes. Are you coming to see our father?"

"I had thought of it, but I will not disturb him now. And," said Athils, sharply, "perhaps I am not wanted when you have secrets with him."

"If it were my choice, I would keep no secrets from you, but—you will hear it all when Frodi wishes," said Thorgeir. "Let me go. I am empty, and I can still feel my legs run under me."

Athils stood aside to let him pass, still smiling, but coldly and without mirth.

The High Moot consisted of councillors from every town and village, apportioned at one member for every fifty people. Some had stayed with friends or relations in Velir, but most had camped in and around the Assembly ground, and all had, of course, brought their own provisions, or Velir would have gone hungry to feed them. The last comers, those from the farthest places, Imma, Langt, and distant Sidastur which lay on the very shore of the Sea, had arrived during the afternoon of the fifth day, that day on which Thorgeir also reached home. Early on the following morning, the whole Moot gathered around a platform which had been set up in the middle of the Assembly ground, high enough so that any who wished to speak could be seen and heard. There were eighty or more of them gathered there, men and women, old and young, and around the edges of the field in respectful silence many of the folk of Velir stood or sat on the ground to watch. Thorgeir was among them, still befogged with sleep, and Ylga was beside him, her arm around his waist.

He had gone to visit her on his way to the Assembly ground, after breakfast, but had told her nothing but that he was back. She said, now, "You *are* provoking, not to say a word. If you will not tell me what you did and what news you brought Frodi, at least tell me where you got that new sword you are wearing."

"Not now, Ylga," he said. "My father is about to open the Moot. And you will hear it all soon enough."

Frodi had ascended the platform. He held up his hand. Tall as he was, and still taller where he stood, dressed in a green kirtle and black leather trews, his hair and beard carefully combed, he looked the personification of power and dignity.

He said, "The peace of Arveid be upon us, and may she listen to our debates and guide us in our decisions."

"Be it so," they all answered, and thus the Moot was begun.

Frodi said, "We have summoned you to hear grim news, and to decide what should be done. Some of you already know it, for rumor flies quickly, and not all of it near the mark. The plain truth is that the Tyrnings have settled on Nimma's Field half a mile from the edge of the high ground above Esk. They are building cabins of stone, planting kala-beans, digging wells. They have brought water and provisions with them and clearly they hope to stay through the next winter and to make steadings for themselves. The council of Velir know this because a report was brought to us by my son, Athils, who went and spied out their doings. Now, we must—"

He was interrupted by the Speaker from Havarda, a hale ld man with a gray beard spreading like a fan on his broad hest. "You go too fast, Frodi. You say they hope to stay nrough the winter. They are digging wells, are they? But nere is no water on Nimma's Field except what a man makes imself. A child can see they do not plan to stay there."

A mutter of agreement went up, and knots of people egan arguing loudly among themselves. Frodi called above ne noise, "Let me finish!" They fell quiet, and he stared about im, quelling them with his gaze.

Then he went on, "Everyone may speak, but let us speak n turn or we will end by deafening ourselves with shouting. ut first, do not think I am such a simpleton as to believe they nean no harm. What I think, I will tell you in due time. But do ot be hasty! Do not rush into war without first considering vhat can be done to keep peace."

Svip Leaper had held up his hand, and he now climbed aboriously on the platform. "I, too, have something to say efore we begin the real meat of the talk. For Frodi began by aying that there had been rumors far from the truth. Let us et at the truth, by all means. Frodi has been modest. His son, thils, went at great risk to spy upon the Tyrnings and made a vonderful run home again to warn us of their doings on Nimma's Field. But Frodi has two sons." Shading his eyes, he ooked about, and pointed at Thorgeir, where he stood on the dge of the field. "There stands his other son, Red Thorgeir." hen, abruptly changing his tone, he bellowed, "Now, answer ne this, Frodi—where did Thorgeir get the belt and sword he

wears, the belt which is buckled with the sign of the Demo
Woman?"

Heads turned, people craned to stare, a babble of voice
broke out. Several of the councillors who were neares
Thorgeir stepped forward to see him better, and one, a youn
man with tow-colored hair, shouted to Svip, "What sign?"

"Shears! Is not the buckle in the shape of a pair o
shears?" Svip answered.

"It's true."

"The shears are the sign the Tyrnings use for their Devil
Arveid. I know, and so do some others who have gone t
bargain with them at the Midyear Market. Ask Disa Black
tooth, there, or Bjarni Wryneck from Hamvir."

The faces that regarded Thorgeir darkened with hostilit
and suspicion. Then they turned away from him to hear more

Frodi was trying to say something, but Svip elbowed hin
back and went on in his bull's voice, "I have not done. It is m
right to speak. Everyone in Velir knows that young Thorgeir i
too soft by far, that he is a lover of the Detestable People—yes
that his own faith is weak. Like father, like son. I will tell yo
where the sword came from. Frodi sent Thorgeir to talk pri
vately with the Tyrnings. Is that the truth, Frodi, or isn't it?"

For once, Frodi seemed at a loss. "I will explain—" h
began.

"Is it not true that a Tyrning gave Thorgeir that sword?"
cried Svip.

"Answer! Answer!" shouted some of the crowd.

Frodi's neck swelled, and his face reddened with anger. "Yes," he said, at last, striving to control himself. "But will ou—"

He could say no more, for his voice was drowned in the uproar. Here and there, hands went to weapons, but no sword was drawn, for it was a crime to bare a weapon at the Moot.

Svip's voice cut through the noise. "Treachery! You have not heard it all." They became quiet, to listen. "In our council, when the bold Athils brought us the news that the Tyrnings had settled on Nimma's Field, Frodi urged us to bargain with them. One swift troop of warriors would have ended the matter, but he refused to fight them. Ask the other councillors. They will bear me out. Now we know why. It was because he wanted time to warn his friends, those murderers of babes, those worshipers of the devil. That very day, Frodi sent his other son, Thorgeir, on a journey to the Detestable People, to carry word to them that we knew their plans. One of the Tyrnings was a man named Hjal, another was called Ketl Ari's-son, and it was he who gave Thorgeir the sword and belt as a reward for his services. Deny it if you dare, Frodi. What was to be the reward for your treachery?"

At that, the uproar was deafening. The crowd surged this way and that, fists were shaken, some cried out that Frodi should be put to trial, others that he must be heard. Hands clutched at his ankles to pull him down. Svip, standing back, watched with a smile that was like a snarl. Frodi gave up trying to be heard and half turned to Svip to say something. The

fat man gave him a shove. Frodi's temper, never certain
snapped. Baring his teeth, he drew his sword.

Svip jumped down from the platform, shouting, "Shoot!'

From somewhere, an arrow came whirring over the head
of the councillors. It buried itself in Frodi's chest with a thump
that could be clearly heard across the field. Frodi clutched at it
staggering. A second struck him in the eye, and he fell back
ward from the platform with a yell of agony.

Thorgeir had watched and listened in horror, and when
Frodi drew his sword, he also set his hand to his hilt. But a
that moment, he was pulled backward by Ylga. He saw his fa
ther fall, and at the same time Ylga said in his ear, "Come. No
a word. Quick!"

They were standing not two paces from her garden wall
Everyone's attention was on the platform, where Ragn the
Peacemaker had leaped up and was waving his hands and
calling for silence and order. Svip could not be seen. Thorgei.
still held back, and Ylga whispered, "They will kill you, next.'
At that, he let himself be dragged away.

She gave him a push. "Over the wall," she said.

On the other side of it, she led the way, running at a
crouch in through the rear door of the house. Inside, she
paused long enough to take down a light knapsack that hung
from a peg; it was her own, which she used when she went
hunting. She hastened to the front door, and peered out. With
a jerk of her head, she motioned Thorgeir to follow. The
street was still empty, although they could hear the voices in

the Assembly ground. They sped to the other end of the town. There, where the path ascended the hill to the selva fields, was a tumbledown shack. It had belonged to a man named Hrafn Threefingers, who had had no luck. Everything went wrong with him, and in the end he had fallen from the roof while repairing a hole, and had broken his neck. Since then, the house had been left empty, and children said it was haunted and dared each other to go inside. Ylga entered it with Thorgeir close behind.

She said, "You must stay here until nightfall. And then—"

"And then I will find the man who shot those arrows, and kill him," Thorgeir said, between his teeth. "And Svip as well."

"You will do better to think of saving your own life," said Ylga, sternly. Then tears came into her eyes, and she put her arms around him. "Oh, Thorgeir, how much truth was there in what Svip said? You would not tell me where you got the sword."

"Do you think so ill of me, too?" he said. "Do you believe my father and I were traitors?"

"I think only that Svip had everything planned for Frodi's death, and he will not stop at that. There will be another arrow for you."

He groaned. "I swear to you there was no treachery. It is true my father had a friend who is a Tyrning. He sent me to see if war might be avoided. I was befriended there, among

the Tyrnings, when my life was threatened, and one of them
gave me this sword."

She looked at him in the gloom of the empty house, and
touched his cheek. "Arveid knows I believe you acted for the
best," she said. "But I do not understand."

"Well, all is over, now," said he. "Svip and his friends
will be searching for me. No one must see you. Tonight, I will
try to slip out of the town."

"Do not go before I return. I will talk to Bera Agni's-
daughter. She was always your father's friend. She will not
lightly see you slain. Promise you will do nothing until I come
again."

He nodded, and she went out cautiously.

All that day he lay hidden in the darkest corner of the hut.
There was bread and cheese in the knapsack she had left with
him, and a leather bottle of water, but he had no appetite. At
first, his thoughts were all of his father: Frodi alive, the tallest
man in a room, his booming laugh, his gusto in eating and
drinking, his swiftness of decision, his great strength, his gentleness when Thorgeir and Athils were children. He had
taught them patiently how to wield weapons; he had run beside them, as they learned their paces. And then Thorgeir saw
him staggering with the arrow in his chest, falling in anguish.
How had it happened? How had Svip come to learn so much
about Thorgeir's errand, about the sword, even the names of
Hjal and Ketl?

He turned the matter over and over in his mind. Someone

had spied upon him, that was the only conclusion he could come to. And inevitably, thinking back upon all that had happened, he remembered Athils outside the door, upon the stair.

"My own brother?" he thought. There could be no other explanation. Athils must have seen him return, must have lurked outside the room and listened. He had heard everything, and had gone to Svip hoping to gain credit. Athils' ambition was clear: he wanted to be war captain. Perhaps he had not realized that it would come to Frodi's death, for Athils was far from subtle. He had wished only to push the issue to a decision for war. But Svip had had his own plans.

The deep and piercing pain of this understanding drove all other thoughts out of Thorgeir's mind. He lay numbly, his head on his arms, and after a time he slept in the dust.

It was the middle part of the night, when he awoke, and for an instant he thought he was back in the forest with the ylvan, for the situation was the same, darkness and a touch on his face. Then Ylga's whisper came: "Thorgeir?"

"Yes?"

"Come with me, there is someone who wants to see you."

He was ready and alert at once. They crept out of the house and through the silent streets. They came to the long, rambling house where the councillor, Bera Agni's-daughter, dwelt, and Ylga scratched lightly on the door. It was opened almost at once by Bera herself, holding a flickering oil lamp. She closed the door behind them, and beckoned them to follow. She brought them through the hall and beyond, into a small inner chamber with tight-shuttered windows. Three more lamps in a stand lighted it, and Ragn the Peacemaker sat there, at a table, with his chin on his fist.

He stood, and came round to clasp Thorgeir by the hand.

"I sorrow with you for Frodi's death," said he. "It was evilly plotted. But at least we have you safe, thanks to Ylga's quickness."

"I saw how matters were going," Ylga said. "But it was Bera who gained time for you by telling everyone she had seen you running eastward, toward Vapnwood."

Thorgeir turned to Bera. Her eyes, usually full of lively mockery, were dull and rimmed with red from much weeping, and her handsome face showed deep lines and was pale in the smoky light. She put down the lamp she had been carrying, and with the back of a hand brushed the long hair out of her eyes.

"I loved your father," she said. "I would have wedded him if he had wished it."

Thorgeir pressed her hand.

"It was well that Ylga came to me," Bera said. "We asked her to bring you here because there is much to talk of. And first, how came Svip to know of your journey to Hjal Broadbiter?"

Thorgeir started. He glanced from her to Ragn, and said, "Did *you* know of it?"

Ragn nodded. "We two were trusted by Frodi. We have long known about your father's blood brother. And we have told Ylga, so that she might know how guiltless you are."

"You know everything, then? This sword and belt—"

"We met with Frodi last night," said Ragn. "He told us all."

"Yet not quite everything," Thorgeir said, bitterly. "I have been thinking how Svip could know as much as he did, and now I am sure of the answer. It was my brother's doing."

"Athils!" Bera exclaimed. "No, you must be wrong, for Frodi told us he was careful not to speak of it to Athils."

Thorgeir told how he had met his brother on the stair outside Frodi's study. "He had been listening at the door," he said. "He must have gone to Svip with what he heard. My brother!" He ground his teeth. "I swore to kill the man who shot my father, but how can I slay my own brother? Yet he is as guilty of our father's death as if he had drawn the bow himself."

"Do not think of revenge, now," Bera said, gently. "I have tasted it, and it is a sour dish to sup on, with little nourishment in it."

Thorgeir was struck by another thought. "There was something else he must have heard, as well—"

"Yes," said Ragn, in a somber tone. "The kraken." He stood in thought, twisting up the points of his moustache, with his head bowed, and went on, "Let us all sit down, and Bera, give us something to drink, for 'A dry throat utters dull counsel.' "

Ylga sat close beside Thorgeir on a bench and said to him, in an undertone, "The kraken? What does he mean? I am all astray."

In a few words, while Bera fetched ale and ale horns, he told her. His explanation left her more confused than before.

"The ylvan?" she said. "The kraken? You might as well tell me that Budri Brightface is coming, or that the Midgard Serpent has been found."

"Nevertheless, it is the truth," Ragn said. "And Bera and I know it to be so."

He drank deeply, wiped his moustache with his palm and continued, "I told you that last night we met with Frodi. He told us of your return from Hjal and also of how you had met the ylvan. We, too, Ylga, could not believe altogether in that strange tale—the beast's warning that the kraken was coming. No, even though we knew how trustworthy Thorgeir was, for he might have dreamed it all. But Frodi had waiting in the house below, the spaeman, Gunnlaug. He went down and fetched him, brought him up to the study and bade him look into the future to see if there was anything to be seen there concerning the kraken.

"Then Gunnlaug brought out paper, pen and ink, and sat down at the table before us and fell into a sleep, and while he slept his hand drew this picture."

He took from the wallet at his belt a piece of paper, unfolded it, and laid it on the table before them. Thorgeir bent to look, and felt a thrill run up his spine. On the paper was drawn a wide, flapping shape rising above tiny trees, the shape the ylvan had shown him in his mind's eye.

"I can see," said Ragn, "that you recognize it. We roused

Gunnlaug and showed him what he had drawn, and asked
him if there was more to be said. And he spoke a stave:

> *Far is that place   and hard the faring*
> *Where Illthorn grows   in icy ground.*
> *There must he walk   the weapon-wielder,*
> *In Arveid's heart   let hero seek.*

"No more would he say, but took his fee and departed, as
is the way of the spaefolk. But we had seen enough to know
that the warning given to Thorgeir was no dream.

"We debated the matter, trying to decide what to do.
Clearly, if such a monster as this is coming, it endangers us
all, both Tyrnings and Vollings, for it will make no distinction
between one side and the other. All selva fields alike will be
food for it. In the face of such a threat our war fades to noth-
ingness. But how to persuade the folk of the danger?

"In the end, we agreed that nothing could be done to stop
the Moot, and that the question of the Tyrnings on Nimma's
Field must be discussed first. Frodi felt sure the majority
would vote for negotiation, and indeed, but for Svip, they
would have done so. Then Frodi planned to call together the
Speakers of every council this very night, and bring Gunnlaug
the Spaeman before them. He felt that a smaller group would
listen to reason, where a larger one might be pulled in too
many ways. Perhaps we might ask the Tyrnings to join with
us in sending out a scouting party, to find the kraken and

see it for themselves so that we might know how to fight it.

"But that," he finished, "is all hopeless, now."

"Why so?" Thorgeir demanded. "Why can you not call together the Speakers? You have the picture Gunnlaug made—"

"Because Svip knew too much and moved too swiftly," answered Bera. "Had that story not come out today, Frodi would have told the Speakers of it in his own time, candidly. But now, Svip has the mastery. He has made it seem that everything Frodi did and said was pure treason. The mood now is all for war. Do you not know Svip's hatred? For him, unbelievers are a greater enemy than any other. He is blind to everything but that. If we came forward now with this tale—that a creature of myth is coming to threaten us— he would laugh at us, he would call us traitors, too, and say that we paid Gunnlaug to help us spread so fantastic a tale. Even a spaeman may be bribed. And it *is* fantastic! If I did not know you, Thorgeir, and your father, even I might doubt it."

She struck her palms together. "If only Frodi had not let himself be goaded into drawing his sword!" she finished.

They sat without a word, for a time, and then Ylga said, rather timidly, "If it is true that the kraken exists, and that it is returning to destroy us—then the rest of the tale of Budri must be true, also."

The others stared at her. Ragn sucked in a breath, and said, sharply, "Yes? Go on."

"It must be true that once before it came, and was destroyed by Arveid's help. The spaeman said it—someone must do as Budri did, and go to the Temple of Arveid to ask Her help. 'Where Illthorn grows.' That is where Budri went in the saga."

" 'East of the sun and west of the moon?' " said Bera, with a touch of her old mockery.

Ragn sat suddenly erect, and seemed about to speak.

But Thorgeir, full of excitement, broke in, "Why not? The saga says he went to the land beyond the north wind. There, in the north, lies the ice—the spaeman said, 'In icy ground.' And he said also, 'In Arveid's heart.' Where else would that be but in Her temple? Her temple exists, it is there, somewhere, for I heard among the Tyrnings that one of them once found it."

He struck the table with his fist. "If part of the old tale is true, why not all of it? Ylga is right. Why should there not be weapons to be had from the Goddess's hand, as the saga says?"

He sprang to his feet. "If I may not take revenge on Athils for our father's death, I will no longer mourn. I will go. I take oath for Frodi's sake that I will find the temple, and beg weapons of the Maiden."

Bera ran her fingers through her hair. "It is madness," she said. "And yet you cannot stay here, for they have already cried you an outlaw. But I—" She caught her breath. "I believe in the Goddess with all my heart, and yet I cannot believe that the temple lies there for the finding. I do not know what to believe."

"Then listen," Ragn put in. "A while ago, you laughed

when you said, 'East of the sun and west of the moon.' I know something of the northland, for in my youth I led raiding parties over Boldneb Pass, and explored the land nearly to the range of Goldcrest looking for a way to attack the Tyrning's steadings near Breita. In that land above Breita, which is the most northerly of the Tyrnings' settlements, you can see still farther to the north two peaks standing before Goldcrest itself. On old maps, that on the west, or left hand, is called the Wife of Glenr, and that on the east, or right hand, is called the Mirror of Gefjun. Now, Bera, you know the art of poesy and you have read the Book of the Skalds. What do those names mean in the kenning of poets?''

Bera bit her lip. ''The Wife of Glenr is the sun, and the Mirror of Gefjun is the moon.''

''Just so. To reach Goldcrest Mountain, therefore, one must go east of the sun and west of the moon—between those two peaks. So there is one more truth in the saga.''

He clapped a hand on Thorgeir's shoulder. ''Go, then,'' he said. ''It will take courage and luck, but I know you have the one, and since you are still alive maybe you have the other as well.''

''I will go this very night, at once,'' said Thorgeir.

''You will not go alone, then,'' Ylga said.

He regarded her with surprise, beginning to ask why not, then understanding. ''You?'' he said. ''You would leave your family, your friends, Velir, to go with me on a search that may only end in death?''

"All going or staying ends some time or other in death," said Ylga. "And I had rather go with you than wait behind."

She stood up, decisively, and took his hand. "Ragn," she said, "you are a priest of Udi. We have no rings to exchange, nor bridal gifts to make. But before you, I vow that I will take Thorgeir Frodi's-son as my husband and share his fate."

She looked into Thorgeir's mismatched eyes, a smile on her lips. "And you?" she said. "Or will you not have me?"

"I vow to take Ylga Olof's-daughter as my wife," said Thorgeir, "and share her fate. And it is more than I dared to hope for. Do not change your mind, Ylga."

She laughed, and they embraced, while Bera and Ragn watched, smiling.

Bera said, "I will give you bridal gifts suited to your condition—knapsacks and provisions. I will give you weapons as well, for I do not think Ylga should take the chance of going home. The sooner you leave the better, while it is yet dark."

"I have no gift for you," said Ragn, "except to ask Udi and Arveid to protect you. Remember, the lives of us all, Vollings and Tyrnings, may be in your hands. Let nothing delay you! As for your way, I will draw you a map."

Bera gave him pen and paper from a chest, and went off to pack up food and drink. Ylga, too, took paper and wrote a note to her parents, asking their forgiveness and saying that she loved Thorgeir and was following him into outlawry. Very soon, all was ready for their departure. In addition to knapsacks stuffed with food and necessities, Bera gave them some spare clothing, bows, quivers of arrows, and hunting knives. They girded themselves and stood before Ragn, whose map was ready.

He laid a finger on it, tracing their route. "My advice to you," he said, "is to go from here to Brekka and then turn north, crossing the open land and avoiding Imma, and making straight for the pass of Boldneb. Beyond that pass go north and you will see the two peaks of the sun and the moon rising in the distance, and beyond them, Goldcrest. If the temple of Arveid lies anywhere, it will be beyond that last mountain."

Thorgeir nodded. He took the map and tucked it into his belt wallet. He and Ylga made their farewells, embracing Bera and Ragn in the knowledge that they might never meet again. Bera led them to the door. It had seemed to Thorgeir that they were inside the house for hours, but only a short time had passed and the night still lay heavy and silent, the stars of the Ale Horn giving a pale luminosity in the streets. Ylga's night vision was better than Thorgeir's, and she went confidently ahead. As softly as smoke drifting, they left the town and took the western road, that same way Thorgeir had gone when he began his run only six days before.

Alternately trotting and walking, they put eight miles between themselves and Velir. They were walking, side by side, the last mile or so before the hamlet of Brekka, when Thorgeir reached for Ylga's hand.

"It has just come to me that we are wed," he said. "I wish that my father could have known it."

"Perhaps he knows, in the Land of Shadow." The Vollings believed that the dead waited for the day on which Udi would end the earth and make them immortal in a new world.

Thorgeir said, "The dead know nothing. That river between their land and ours is too wide for speech. Perhaps it is better so. He would know, too, of my brother's evil deed."

She squeezed his fingers. "Do not grieve," she said. "It can do no good."

"I know that. It is the last you will hear of it. I will turn myself to what has to be done—and to you."

The wide dusty road was white before them in the starlight, and by its reflection he could see her eyes flash as she glanced at him. Desire rose in him. Their bodies were not strangers, for among the Vollings and Tyrnings alike, young people made love to each other whenever they wished before making the formal contract of exchanging rings, vows, and the settlement of property. Many times during the past year, Thorgeir and Ylga had gone privately into the forest together, but now he looked at her as if for the first time.

He caught her in his arms and kissed her tenderly.

"Not now," she said, after a moment. "We must be far from any pursuit before we stop to rest. Remember what Ragn said."

"No one will pursue us. Svip will have his way and my brother will be glad to have seen the last of me. But let it be as you say."

Nevertheless, he kissed her once again. With her hands

on his arms, she said, "Even if the temple of Arveid is no more than a tale, even if we perish in the north, I am contented."

"We will find it," he said, firmly. "It is there, somewhere."

"You said that a Tyrning had found it once."

"Yes, and brought something back from it. I have it, something old and magical. It was given to me by my father. Its twin is worn by a man named Orm, my blood brother, a Tyrning. I do not know whether Ragn told you of him."

As he spoke, he reached into his shirt to touch the amulet that hung round his neck. "It is too dark to see it properly, but here—you can feel it," he said, drawing it forth. "It is like nothing I have—"

Her cry stopped him. But in the same instant he saw it for himself, a small, bright disk of light like one of the glowing stars of the Ale Horn in his hand.

"Orm!" he said.

V

EAST OF THE SUN
AND WEST OF THE MOON

FOR a moment, Thorgeir was so bewildered that he forgot everything and could think only of setting off at once to find his friend. He had, indeed, taken a couple of steps with the shining amulet in his hand, when Ylga caught him by the arm.

"What is it?" she cried. "What does it mean?"

"I will tell you as we go," he said. "But first, I must let him know that I have seen his signal."

He fumbled at the side of the amulet until he felt the small projecting blue stone under his finger, and pressed it as he had been told. It went in and remained there, flush with the surface. He tucked the amulet away again, inside his shirt.

"Let us hurry," he said. "This amulet is one of a pair which were brought from Arveid's temple by an ancestor of that friend of my father's, Hjal Broadbiter. It was given me by Orm Handskill, a man you will love, Ylga. He is upright and full of honor, brave and modest, and he stood by me when there were some who would have slain me. The magic of this thing is that if one of us is in trouble, the amulet will shine as you have seen. It can only mean that something has happened to Orm. He needs me, and I must go to him."

"But where?"

"We have settled a meeting place, south of here, on the shoulder of Blackfell."

"South?" She halted in her tracks. "Wait, Thorgeir! We cannot go there. Remember what Ragn said. Our road lies north, and we must hasten."

He stopped, irresolute. Then he said, "Ylga, if the ground were to be split open for it, I yet could not break the oath of blood brotherhood. What good is there in faithfulness, if one begins by being unfaithful to one's friend? When we come to Brekka, do you turn north. I will run all night, for I know the way, and tomorrow if luck is with me I will find Orm and learn his need. I will follow you after that, and with Udi's help I will find you again, somehow. If not, you must try to find the temple."

He heard her breath catch in a sob. She said, "And shall I begin with unfaithfulness as well? I swore to share your fate. But what of the faith we must keep with Ragn and Bera and the others?"

"I swore no oath to them. I will go north when I have found Orm," he replied, stubbornly.

"I will go with you, then, but I do not know whether you are right or wrong."

"Only Udi knows that. Let us be moving then, for the sooner we find him, the sooner we can return."

In spite of his urgency, however, they could not go on for long, for once they had left the main road at Brekka it was too dark to run cross-country steadily, and they soon saw that they would make better time in the daylight. They were also more burdened than Thorgeir had been when first he had made this journey. Some miles beyond Brekka, therefore, in the lee of a hillock, among low bushes covered with sweet-smelling flowers, they slept with one of their sleeping-cloths below them and the other above, warm in each other's arms. The brightening sky, the light dew on their faces, awoke them; they said their morning prayers, hand in hand, broke their fast, and set out. Thorgeir, remembering this rolling ground, estimated that they had perhaps another twenty-five miles to cover. They ran at the easy lope used by raiding parties when laden with camping gear and weapons, slow-seeming but steadily eating up the distance. They had started early, and so, although they rested every hour and gave themselves a longer rest and a mouthful of water late in the morning, it was early afternoon when they saw before them the bare rocky knoll rearing beneath the precipices of Blackfell.

They found Orm lying on a bed of moss with his back against a rock. At their approach, a fat gray lizard with a cruel-looking beak, a creature longer than Thorgeir's arm, which had been watching a short distance away, turned with a flop and scuttled out of sight. It was a tyggja, a carrion eater. Its presence was not to be wondered at, for Orm was gray faced and haggard, and blood stained his left side and had clotted on his cheek and chin. He wore nothing but cross-gartered breeches and shoes, and the sword Thorgeir had given him lay beside him.

He smiled wanly as they approached, and said, in a faint voice, "Alas, you have frightened away my dinner, for if it had come closer I would have eaten it. I hope you have brought something in its place."

Thorgeir could not smile in return. He and Ylga knelt beside Orm, and Ylga opened her pack and began emptying it.

"What has happened? Where are you wounded?" Thorgeir asked.

"Nothing much. A cut across the chest and one on the cheek," said Orm. "But I have lost much blood, and have come far, and I have had neither food nor drink since yesterday."

Ylga had found a small pot of healing ointment which Bera had put into her pack, and she was already cutting a shirt into strips with her hunting knife.

"We will have to use some of our water," she said briskly, "for his wound must be cleaned and bandaged."

Orm said, "Had I known Thorgeir would bring you, I would have summoned him sooner."

"She is Ylga Olof's-daughter, my—wife," said Thorgeir, stumbling a little over the word.

"May you both be fortunate and happy," Orm said, weakly. He laid his head back and closed his eyes, and they let him rest while Ylga washed the slash across his chest, smeared it with ointment and bandaged it skillfully. It had divided the muscles but had not gone deep. As for the cut on his cheek, although like all face wounds it had bled profusely, it needed only to be left alone to heal.

Thorgeir got out some dried meat and biscuit and when Orm seemed comfortable, gave him a little at a time, cutting the meat into thin slices and breaking up the biscuit. He gained in strength under their eyes as he ate, and soon sat up, wincing, and asked for more.

"Tell us what happened," Thorgeir said.

"It was Oli and his friends," said Orm. "Do you remember them?"

"Of course. The three we fought with."

"Others of their gang had gone farther along the Modru road. When they saw that they had missed us, they returned and met Oli. They went back to Liskhavn and gathered more young men and women. That night, Ketl came to warn Hjal that the town was rousing in anger against him, that Oli was saying he and Gerda were no other than secret heretics themselves and in league with the Vollingfolk. I, too, was not forgotten; I was with you that night, you remember, and they said I had gone off with you to join your people and tell them our plans.

"But my uncle is a stubborn man and would not believe that his own neighbors would go against the law. If they wished, said he, they could bring him to trial, otherwise he would not heed the snapping and slinking of a few young carrion lizards." He hesitated, and then said, "*Was* a stubborn man, I should have said."

"He is dead?" Thorgeir said, gently.

Orm nodded. "I returned next day and found crowds gathering in the streets. I got black looks, and there was some cursing and stone throwing, but nothing more. We slept upon our weapons in the hall, and early in the morning we smelled the smoke—they had set fire to the house. They would not come bravely against us. Hjal said he would not lift a sword against his own people. He and Gerda sat down in their high seats in the hall, and there they waited calmly for death. But I broke forth with the servants and kemperymen and we found a little good work to do. Luck was with me; I met Oli and left my mark on him."

"You slew him?"

"No, I do not kill men if I can help it. I cut off his right hand. He will not be so ready to strike at strangers from now on. Then I burst through the mob and got away. I came here, for I knew the cry would be out against me and I could hope for nothing better than outlawry, for," he added, his lips curling in scorn, "there is no hatred like that which goes with love of the Maiden."

"That is true among us Vollings as well, and I am a victim of it, like you," said Thorgeir.

He told Orm all his tale, beginning with the meeting with the ylvan. Orm listened in wonder.

When Thorgeir had done, he said to Ylga, "You were right, and although I would have done as Thorgeir did, he was wrong. Finding Arveid's temple is more important than my skin."

She had been watching him with increasing approval, and now she smiled at him. "Still, I do not regret it."

"You may yet," he replied, "for I intend to go with you both."

"Can you walk?" Thorgeir said.

"Walking is the cure for all ills save death," said Orm, "and maybe even that. Get me on my feet."

They helped him rise, slowly, and he stamped first one foot, then the other.

"Now, give me a drop of water to drink," said he.

When they had done so, he said, "I am ready. Today, let us go slowly, but tomorrow I will run not far behind."

Thorgeir had another shirt in his knapsack, and he helped Orm put it on. Then he brought out Ragn's map and they all three studied it.

"It appears to me," Ylga said, "that from here, instead of returning to Brekka, if we follow the skirts of the mountains we can cross the Pass of Voll. On the Tyrnings' side the going will be easier, and we can then strike north-northwest for those two peaks that lie before Goldcrest."

"You are right," said Thorgeir. "It is what we will do."

The days that followed were hard and long. Despite Orm's insistence, he was not able to run the next day, and they had to walk across the long, sloping spurs that ran off from Black-fell Ridge. However, he grew stronger and his wound mended quickly; by the third day, he was able to trot for some miles between longer marches, and neither Thorgeir nor Ylga showed any of their impatience.

Blackfell Ridge gave way to the forest-clothed heights of Hugin and Munin, twin peaks of gray rock. The lower parts of the forest were mostly golden askas, their trailing leaves dancing and shimmering as the light breeze tossed them, a heart-lifting sight. Orm found a straight sapling, as tall as himself and two fingers thick, with a fork at the top. This he trimmed to make himself a staff. At Thorgeir's request, he later found another, and thereafter, every morning and evening, they practiced together, Orm teaching his friend attack, defense and how to disarm an opponent with the forked end. At first, Thorgeir had to bear sharp raps and bruises, but as time passed he became better able to hold his own.

Slowed as they were by Orm's recovery, they came on the morning of the fourth day to the Pass of Voll, a wide gap between low but steep hills. They crossed by the Old High Road and branched off it into a lovely wooded vale full of blossoming shrubs and tall-stemmed scented grasses. They traveled north along it for two days, trotting steadily, but forced to spend some time each day hunting, for their provisions were dwindling and Thorgeir insisted they should save some for a more barren time. The valley was full of small game, but it was shy as if much hunted, and indeed they were not far from the

towns of Vagn and Austastur with their hamlets and steadings. Yet they never saw another person, and Ylga's craft as a
hunter kept them fed. A few tiny streams crossed the vale, so
that they were never short of water.

But this pleasant interval was soon over. The ranges of
Baldrock and Boldneb had fallen away to the right, but ahead
of them new mountains rose, their bare pinnacles purple
against the sky. Clear to be seen were those two peaks of
which Ragn had told them, the Wife of Glenr and the Mirror
of Gefjun. Behind them reared another, its point white in the
sunlight; this was Goldcrest. The vale widened and its green
leafiness gave way to stones and mosses. Game grew scarce
and the streams vanished. The air became colder as the land
lifted, but they dared not build fires lest their smoke be seen,
for they were only a few miles from Breita, the most northerly
of the Tyrnings' towns. Thorgeir made them gather fagots and
tie them to the tops of their packs for later use. In another day,
they had put Breita thirty miles behind them and were in the
wasteland.

It was as if someone had brought vast cartloads of stones
and dumped them in heaps. Hills of stone rose out of the
dusty, pebbly ground, and boulders as big as houses were
scattered between them, intermingled with splinters and slabs
of every size. They were of every color, too; some rose-red and
pink, banded with yellow, some iron-gray and dove-gray, glittering with golden specks, some the dark glassy green of the
sea, some encrusted with white or lavender crystals. Among

them grew leathery plants covered with long spines, and these were a constant menace to the legs of the three, so that their pace was slowed. A sharp wind came and went, piping against the edges of the rocks, sometimes sounding so like the notes of a herdsman's flute that it startled them. But they saw no signs of life.

Now and again, as they trotted along, Thorgeir thought he saw crude markings scratched on the surfaces of rocks, but felt he must be deceived by the veins and markings of color. At last, however, they came to a particularly high, flat face of rock, and he stopped to look more closely. There was no mistaking that a hand had cut three large shapes into the stone. They were like runes, but none that he could read: a tree with five branches, an arrow and a circle with a line through it.

"Someone lives here," he said.

"What does it mean?" said Ylga. "And how can anyone live in this place?"

"Hunters, maybe," Orm said.

"Hunters of stones?"

Thorgeir gazed about. They were standing at the entrance to a canyon. On their left ran that high face on which the signs were cut, and on their right a steep series of ledges formed by brown and orange slabs piled one upon the other like stairs. Straight before them, the passage opened between these two walls, runnning for five hundred paces or more and showing, some distance beyond, a relatively smooth hill dotted with a green too soft to be rock. Several of the thorny plants grew at the entrance, and thirty feet inside another with fewer spines but of monstrous size, its rind mottled and weathered.

"Something is growing on that hill," Orm said. "Not these prickly things, but another sort of plant. And look, surely those are stokkna moving among them?"

He pointed, and the others saw a couple of small, graceful shapes appear for an instant on the top of the hill and then, with a bound, vanish again.

"Let us go," he said. "My mouth waters for fresh meat."

Thorgeir touched his arm. "Wait," he said.

"What's the matter?"

"I don't know. Something misgives me. This is a fit place for an ambush."

Orm stared at the heights on either hand, and shrugged. "Even an ambush would be a change from running," said he.

He shifted his staff to his left hand and drew his sword. Then he stepped forward. Thorgeir snatched at him and dragged him back. Just as he did so, something thumped heavily on the spot where Orm had been.

"Ovinur!" Ylga exclaimed.

It was as if their eyes had been opened. The ovinur always adapted itself to blend into its surroundings, sometimes as a tree stump or a mossy rock, and now they saw that what they had taken for an extraordinarily large thorn-plant was the beast itself. Its head, rather, for as usual it had dug its body into the ground. The top gaped enormously open, lined with inward-curving teeth. Its long tongue, like a muscular rope, was still extended almost to Orm's feet, ending in a weighty bulge, sticky and armed with wicked hooks. This tongue, it now began slowly coiling back into its mouth, while its eyes on their slender stalks that looked like thorns, regarded them evilly.

Orm, who had never seen one of these monsters before, gaped at it in astonishment. But Thorgeir and Ylga had, and Thorgeir said, "Get still further back. I think it will strike again."

They moved hastily, a dozen paces away and just in time, for quicker than any rock lizard the tongue lashed out once more. This time, however, it fell short by six yards.

"That is the limit of its reach," Ylga said.

Thorgeir was already scanning the ground. The wall on their left was vertical and too smooth to be climbed. The steps on the right, after rising in easy stages twice the height of a man, ended in one last outward-leaning face twelve feet high.

"We cannot climb out," Thorgeir said. "We shall have to go back and make our way round."

Orm, gazing at the ovinur and the way beyond it, said, "It galls me to turn away from the thing. It can be no more than twenty-five paces away, an easy bow-shot."

"You would but blunt your arrows," said Thorgeir. "It would be like shooting at the bark of an embla tree."

Ylga, however, had shed her pack and was stringing her bow. "Did you mark where the tongue touched last?" she said. "If you are bold enough to get it to strike again, I think I can do it some harm."

Thorgeir's eyebrows rose. "It is no small matter you ask, but maybe it is worth seeing. What shall I do?"

Ylga colored. "I meant Orm," she said.

Both of them laughed at her, and Thorgeir said, "Never. He has no experience of the beast, and besides his wound will make him slow."

Orm said, "I have no wish to see her made a widow so soon."

"Stand still," said Thorgeir. "Go on, Ylga, what must I do?"

"Go as close as you can to that shining pebble—see yonder? It is a full arm's length from where it struck. But wait until I tell you."

She chose three arrows and, holding them and her bow in her left hand, began to climb up the ledges. She stopped from time to time to glance down at the ovinur, and at last she halted on a narrow shelf where there was just room for her to stand and draw her bow. She drew once, slowly, without an arrow on the string, checking the upper and lower limbs of the bow to be sure they did not touch the rock. Then she nocked a shaft.

"Now!" she said.

Thorgeir walked tensely to the spot she had indicated. He had barely reached it when the movement of the ovinur's mouth warned him and he jumped back. The long tongue whipped out, a livid pink streak, and its end struck the ground before him with such force that he felt the blow in the soles of his feet.

In that three seconds during which the tongue began to coil itself up again, Ylga shot. So rapidly did she loose that there was no more than an eye's blink between each flickering shaft. Straight into the ovinur's wide mouth they flew.

The earth exploded about the base of the creature. Stones flew in all directions as it heaved itself upward, ten feet in the air, a writhing tangle of what seemed thick roots surrounding a slug-colored body like a bleached tree trunk. The tongue uncurled, snapped straight up, fell limply back over the head. More unearthly than anything was its silence, for the creature was as voiceless as a plant.

It remained upright, held by the crumbled walls of the pit it had dug, its mouth still open, its tongue lolling. Ylga climbed hastily down again and ran to Thorgeir who caught her tight.

"That was such shooting as I never hoped to see," he said.

Orm patted her on the shoulder, smiling broadly. "By Udi, you must give me lessons. Thorgeir, you will not part with her, will you?"

"Not yet a while," Thorgeir said. "I never thought the ovinur could be slain with arrows."

"It is not dead," said Ylga, "but it soon will be. Old Durid, who taught me to hunt, told me how to deal with it. We met one once, some years ago. The thing has two brains, and that one which controls its head lies above the roof of the mouth. It is none so hard a shot—"

"Ah, she is modest, as well," cried Orm. "I like her more and more. Come, Thorgeir, I will give you a gold chain for her . . . when we return," he added, with a touch of sadness.

They now set forth into the canyon, and although they knew the ovinur could no longer harm them, they nevertheless all three walked gingerly past it, watching it over their shoulders. The ground rose beyond the canyon, and they toiled upward, coming at length to that hill they had seen, smooth and conical. It was so regular as to look like a work of men. It was dotted with vegetation, globular plants with many soft, dark green leaves folded in upon each other in layers. From the center of each bunch a single, tall spike of a green that was nearly black thrust up. At the tip of each spike was a cluster of small white disks on hairlike stems, and when the wind touched them they fluttered wildly, with a faint, fine, musical chiming. Many of the leaves were nibbled, and among the plants were scattered the droppings of the stokkna.

"So we know what the ovinur found to feed on," said Ylga, "for the stokkna must now and then run through the canyon."

Their approach had driven off the shy, fleet animals for the time, but at Ylga's direction they separated near the top of the hill and lay flat to wait. Half an hour later, Thorgeir had shot a young buck. They ate the liver raw for its strength, cut up the rest of the meat and carried it with them until evening, when they made their camp. Thanks to Thorgeir's foresight, they had just enough wood to build a good fire. They heated

stones and toasted many thin strips of meat, which fed them
well that night and left enough for two days' light rations besides, for in that cold air the cooked meat would keep well.

They divided all the spare clothing and put it on. They
nestled close together for more warmth, and in the morning
climbed up upon a great boulder to survey the way ahead.
They were now among the foothills of the range, and on either
hand the two peaks of the sun and moon rose up in jagged
horns. The way between was all broken rock, high cliffs and
gloomy crags. Orm, who had been a climber from his childhood, shook his head.

"Not easily will we go over," said he. "We must look to
creep between, like mice."

And now there was no more trotting, but hard walking,
and clambering and scrambling upward. The only good thing
was that they found the skirts of the mountains were all shattered and cracked so that they could make their way through
narrow gorges, sometimes no more than a dozen paces across,
but passable. Pale, sickly stalks grew in these gorges, clinging
to the bare rock with thin rootlets and lifting brittle branches
high overhead. There were no leaves on the branches, but
bunches of fine bristles, translucent and the color of watery
milk.

Higher they went, and higher, until the great boulders on
the plain below were smaller than pebbles. Frowning above
them, glimpsed through the rifts in the mountains, loomed
Goldcrest, its mighty point covered with frozen snow. The

gorges they climbed in were shadowed except when the sun was at its highest, and the keen wind found its way around corners of rock. Lightly clad as they were, it chilled them so that they felt they never would be warm again. Two days they climbed, and at night they huddled together in crevices, wrapping the two sleeping-cloths tightly around them to keep the wind out.

The lack of water was even worse than the cold, for by the evening of the second day, although they had been very sparing, the two bottles they had with them were empty. The next morning, they slowly chewed the last of their meat, and then their provisions, too, were at an end.

All this time, Thorgeir had kept their spirits up with his resolution. He was no war captain as his brother, Athils, was, but he had the strong, calm purpose and wider view of such a leader as his father had been. Now, however, looking ahead to yet another gully along which they must go, his determination almost faltered.

Orm said, "If we do not come to the end of this soon, we are finished. It is too late to turn back. At any rate, it is more cheering to die in company than alone."

"We must not talk of dying," said Ylga. She turned to Thorgeir. "Shall I not make a scout? I am the swiftest of us."

He shook his head. "We will not part."

"Thorgeir," she said, and took his hand, "is there indeed a temple? Or have we made this journey for nothing?"

"It is there!" he replied, fiercely. "I know it. Nor shall I die before I come to it. Budri Brightface found it, and was alone. These amulets Orm and I wear about our necks tell us that Bjarni the Tyrning found it, and he, too, went alone. Where they went, we can follow. Or are we three friends weaker than they?"

He stood up and drew a deep breath. " 'In trouble and woe to the end of time/Women and men to the world are born,' " he said, quoting from the ancient tale of Brynhild, but turning it into a jest with a smile. "Ylga, wrap one of the sleeping-cloths about you. It will give you some warmth. Orm, you take the other, for the wind may bite your wound and reopen it."

So firm and assured was his tone that they obeyed without question. He took up his pack, much lighter now, and led the way.

That gully proved to be the last. It narrowed until it was hardly more than a crack between two sheer faces, and they came out of it to find themselves at the head of a col, a broad neck which dipped downward before them and ascended again to join one of the outflung buttresses of Goldcrest. The mountain heaved itself hugely above them, its hems covered with the treelike stalks, their pallid bristles like a coating of bluish hoarfrost; above, bare precipices of darker rock hung frowning, and higher still long streaks of pure, dazzling snow rose to the summit, turned to gold by the sunlight.

Now Orm stepped forward again to take the lead. At first the going was easy for the rock was broad enough for half a dozen people abreast and almost as smooth as a road. But as it curved up to meet Goldcrest, it narrowed and became broken. They had to scale shelf after shelf, each higher than the other and with less room at its top. Orm had stubbornly clung to his staff all this way, and he looked at it as if minded to throw it away.

Then he said, "I have always found a stick useful. Who knows when I shall come by another?"

He cut a pair of small notches in it near one end, and with a thong tied it on his back, over his shoulder, the notches holding the thong from slipping. In spite of this awkward burden, he climbed nimbly up a last, long crack, and the others followed him to a ledge barely wide enough for their feet. The rock face sloped inward, away from the depths. Orm pressed himself against it like a fly, making his way slowly, inch by inch, along the ledge. It led slowly upward, and with a final scramble he pulled himself to a broader place above. He lay flat and held out a hand so that Ylga could climb up beside him. Thorgeir came last.

They were high upon the mountain's flank. Looking down the way they had come, they could see the gorge across the col from which they had started, far below them, a mere dark line dividing two massy blocks. Southward, on either hand, sprang up the backs of those two mountains between which they had traveled for three days, like ants in the folds of ladies' skirts.

"We have followed a legend," Thorgeir mused. "East of

the sun and west of the moon! When once I heard you, Ylga, tell the tale of Budri, never did I guess that I would walk in his footsteps.''

''We may find the rest of that saga, too,'' said Orm. ''For as I remember it from my childhood, there is a land of red rock, and a lake of ice, and the tree—I cannot remember its name—''

''Illthorn,'' said Ylga. ''And if we are following Budri, someone is following us.''

The others stared at her. ''I have suspected it for some time,'' she said. ''Since we left the place where the ovinur was, I have seen—well, no more than a flicker of movement now and then, out of the corner of my eye. I thought at first it was some kind of small game, something we might hunt for food, but then I began to guess it was someone keeping watch on us. A good tracker, too. Now, I am sure, for I saw a figure down there, in the crack we came out of between the cliffs. It was only for a second, someone stepping forward to look and then vanishing into the shadows again.''

Thorgeir cupped his hands around his eyes and peered down. ''There is no one there now,'' he said, ''but I trust your hunter's craft. Shall we try an ambush?'' He glanced at the sky. A light haze had begun to overcast the blue. He looked at his companions, their faces pinched with cold and hunger. ''I think not. We must press on, and hope to find shelter by nightfall, and some water, if we can.''

They were upon a wide platform jutting from the eastern

side of the mountain. Following it, they entered a forest of the stalks, twenty feet high or more, their bristles interlacing, whispering softly as they brushed against each other. Their trunks were smooth, unlike the bark of trees, almost fleshlike. After a time, they thinned away and the sky could be seen again. It had become the color of dirty wool.

The climbing now was not so taxing, for it was over broken rock with plenty of crevices for hands and feet. But shortly, a fine sleet began to fall, and with it the wind, which had died away somewhat, came up again, driving hard crumbs of ice into their faces. They bent their heads and struggled on. The sleet stung their cheeks, froze in their hair, gathered in the necks of their tunics and the folds of the sleeping-cloths.

Orm grumbled, "If it were snow, we could at least quench our thirst." The next moment, he stopped so abruptly that the others collided with him.

On their right, the rocks dropped steeply away. But on the left, where the mountain towered, they were opposite a sheer scarp, like the rampart of a fortress, and in it, as it were a gateway, the opening of a cave.

"Do you think—?" Orm began, but Thorgeir was already striding to the cave, drawing his sword as he went.

The other two pressed close behind him, their weapons ready as well. Thorgeir halted a step or two inside. Enough light came in by the entrance for him to see that the place was spacious enough so that, almost, the High Moot might have met there. It appeared to be empty. Its walls were smooth, mottled with veins of lusterless scarlet as if streaked with old blood, along which pockets of small crystals grew like clusters of glassy flowers. Toward the back of the cave, the roof sloped down, and there was a curious formation of rock, humped and gnarled, lying too much in the shadow to be seen. But Thorgeir, trying to make it out, felt the hair prickle on the back of his neck.

Ylga said, with a touch of impatience, "Go farther in, out of the wind."

Thorgeir shrugged off his unease and went a little way on. He brushed the sleet from his hair and clothing, but did not yet sheathe his sword.

Orm said, "By the Maiden, it is warm in here. What a blessing!"

Ylga dropped her pack and began rummaging in it. She found a kerchief and began to towel herself with it, skimpy as it was.

"It *is* warm," she said. "Thorgeir, take off your shirt and wring it out. Do not look so wary. I don't like this place any more than you do, but I had rather be here than in the cold."

Thorgeir still stood, squinting toward the back of the cave. "It is light, too," he said. "Lighter than it should be."

Orm had laid by his staff and was shaking out the sleeping-cloth. He looked up and said, "It is the crystals in the walls."

They were glowing, faintly but clearly, with an amber

light which, as Thorgeir watched, strengthened and waxed to a dark golden-yellow like the eyes of a carrion lizard. The cave brightened as if a baleful sun were shining in it; it grew warmer still, although the sleet rattled against the lip of the entrance. At the same time, a noise was heard from the rear of the cave, a soft growling like that of far distant thunder on a hot day, but going on and on.

In that back part, something moved. What they had taken for a rock formation unfolded itself, a vague shape, taller than any man and oddly blurred as if seen through a mist so that it could not be exactly discerned. It seemed, at one moment, to have too many legs; at another, only a single writhing pedestal. It bent and twisted, even its color uncertain. It was like a thing made of solid shadows cast by an unimaginable lamp.

It seemed to grow larger, and with a shock Thorgeir realized that it was coming toward them, slowly, flickeringly, and yet steadily. A thin bright slit, like an eye opening cautiously, appeared in its upper part.

Involuntarily, Thorgeir raised his sword. Tiny golden sparks danced along the blade, and suddenly the weapon was wrenched from his hand and flew clanging across the cave.

"Back!" he snapped, holding his wrist, for his arm was benumbed. "Out of the cave!"

The brightness at the top of the thing increased. A fine line of intolerable white shot out, touched Thorgeir on the forehead and vanished. He tottered blindly, and fell.

Ylga was at his side at once, snarling like a tigress. She

had her long hunting knife in her hand, and she threw it. In midair, it swerved, sparkling, and hit the wall. Again, the white light flashed out, but Ylga was no longer there. She had leaped to one side, and the beam passed by her.

"Orm!" she shouted. "Quick—while it searches for me!"

He had stood undecided, sword in hand, but at her cry he launched himself forward. Ylga dodged to the left, and he came at the thing from the right. The beam shot out again and missed Ylga by a finger's breadth. As it did so, Orm's sword was torn from his grasp by the same invisible force and clattered away.

"So," he said, between clenched teeth, "iron fails. Wood, then!"

The top of the thing shimmered as if in a wave of heat. Its bright slit eye faced him, and more by instinct than design he crouched low. The white beam blinked over his head. He groped along the floor behind him and caught hold of the end of his staff, as Ylga shouted defiantly from the other side to draw the thing's attention. It turned toward her, and as it did so, Orm lunged violently at it, holding his staff in both hands, stabbing with the sharp forked tip at that spot like an eye from which the light appeared.

He felt something solid yield beneath the wood. Only for an instant, and then it was as if he had pressed against a skin which resisted and then gave, bursting as a bladder full of air might burst, but with a horrible screaming which deafened him. Even as the sound rang in the cave, so that Ylga clapped her hands over her ears and sank to her knees, the thing wavered like smoke, and like smoke vanished upward. On the floor was left a greasy deposit, as if some doubtful campfire had burned there.

Orm remained half-crouched, his ears ringing, his staff still outstretched, the fork of it charred and smoking. Slowly, he straightened. As he did so, a shape darted into the cave, swathed in a great gray cloak with a hood, glittering with sleet. So sudden was the apparition that Orm shrank away. The hood was thrown back. A woman with brilliant, slanting black eyes and glossy black hair coiled in a braid on top of her head faced him. For a breath, she stood, and then with a triumphant laugh, she ran to Orm, caught him about the neck and kissed him.

VI

THE OLD RELIGION

 "LADY," said Orm, looking at her in astonishment, "I do not think we have ever met before, but I will wait while you greet me again."

She drew back, with a smile. She could be seen, now, to be no older than Ylga, but more somber looking, more with-drawn. She had a pale, curiously thick skin scarcely reddened from the cold.

"Hail, Slayer of the Hryllir!" she said. "Now is my father avenged." Her language was the same as that of the Tyrnings and Vollings, but with an unfamiliar accent.

Ylga, after no more than a glance at the newcomer, had run to Thorgeir and fallen on her knees beside him. She put her lips to his, her palm to his chest.

"He is still alive," she said, with relief.

"He will live," said the other woman, "for the Hryllir will not eat dead meat. Be thankful that this man was so prompt." And turning again to Orm, she said, "Tell me your name."

"I am Orm Eirik's-son, called Handskill."

She bowed her head. "Have the thanks of Gudrun Hallr's-daughter. As for Hallr, my father, you may see with your own eyes why I thank you."

She went past Orm to the rear of the cave. After a moment, he followed her, though reluctantly. When they came to the spot where the roof sloped down, he saw that there was an opening, a mere blot of darkness until they had come to it and then, slowly, it began to brighten. Gudrun stood patiently while the light increased, and Orm saw that it came from clusters of the same crystals as those in the outer cave. Beyond, there was a second cave, and as it filled with the amber glow, Orm started back with an exclamation of horror.

The floor was heaped with the dead. Some were shriveled like bundles of dry leather, but still recognizable; some were no more than husks with rags of skin clinging to their bones; some were gray skeletons.

Gudrun pointed to one that lay near the entrance. It had once been a tall, powerful man, but now withered, the flesh fallen in so that the bones of his ribs and shoulders showed, his long black hair tangled about a face that was little more than a skull.

"My father, Hallr," Gudrun said.

"I have seen death before," said Orm, "but I have seen enough of this place."

He turned and stumbled back into the larger cave. As Gudrun went with him, the light in the inner cave faded.

Ylga had risen long enough to come and look over their

shoulders. White-faced, she returned to Thorgeir's side, and said, "Was it that thing, that shadowy shape, that killed them?"

"Yes, and would have done so to all three of you if Orm had not been its bane," said Gudrun.

"What was it?"

"It is called the Hryllir, but what it was or where it came from no one knows. What it did, we know: it struck down its prey with a bolt of lightning and then, while the man or woman still lived but lay asleep, it drained them dry, blood, brains and bowels. It will do so no more."

"But why would anyone come into this cave if such a thing lived here?" Orm asked.

Gudrun went to the wall and put her hand on a clump of crystals. "For these. They are a great treasure. Did you not see how, as soon as you came near them, they gave out light and warmth? They will go on doing so for months, as long as a living being is near them, provided they are taken carefully from their places."

Beneath her gray cloak, she wore a supple leather kirtle and leather leggings, and around her waist was belted a long hunting knife. Putting back her cloak, she drew the knife and pried at the clump, biting her lip and frowning with concentration. The crystals came out slowly and she held them on her palm for the others to see. The base of the clump was encased in some dull metal, almost as if made by the hands of men.

"In this land," she said, tucking the crystals away in a

pouch that hung beside the knife, "where there is little cheer, such things as these are beyond price."

She drew her cloak about her, pulling the hood over her head. "I must take this news to my village," she said. "Look—your friend's eyes are open. He will be himself, soon."

Ylga bent over Thorgeir. He blinked once or twice without moving, as if trying to understand where he was. She kissed him, and he smiled weakly, raising one hand a little way.

"Ah, dear heart," Ylga murmured. "I thought I had lost you."

"Not yet," he said, in a faint voice. "What has happened?"

In a few words, Ylga told him. Gudrun, stirring impatiently, said, "I must go. Orm may come with me, for my people will welcome the slayer of the Hryllir. But as for you two—"

Ylga looked up at her. She said, "It was you who followed us, wasn't it?"

"Yes, for a long time. I saw you come to the gully where the ovinur lay hidden. I saw you shoot it—a good shot," she added, thoughtfully.

"Why did you not warn us, then?" There was an edge to Ylga's tone.

"There was a message cut in the rock, the sign of the ovinur, an arrow pointing to it, and a hand open in warning. It is not our fault if you could not read it."

"There was no warning at this cave," Ylga said, angrily.

"You did not stop us from entering. You wanted us to be killed, if not by the ovinur then by this monster. Why? What harm have we done you?"

Gudrun showed no anger in return. She moved a little away, brooding, and then said, "Do you expect my people to love you? It was your folk who drove us away from the warm land long ago, and harried us because we held to the Old Religion. They slew men, women, children and babes at the breast in the town of Breita, where we dwelt, because we would not give up the worship of Sun-Arveid."

Her voice had grown harsh. "And you still come now and then from Breita," she said, "and hunt the stokkna, and when you meet one of our people you slay him. Why should I love you? I hoped the Hryllir would make an end of you as it did my father and many more of my kin."

Thorgeir got to his feet, still shaky, Ylga catching his arm to help him. He said, earnestly, "All that you say is unknown to us. We do not come from Breita, but from much farther south. I swear to you that we have never heard of your people, nor have we ever harmed them, nor do we know who Sun-Arveid is." He looked into Gudrun's face with his mismatched eyes, and smiled his artless smile. "Our errand lies not here but much farther on. Now, we are hungry and in need of shelter and rest. Will you turn us away? I have no hatred of you, nor of anyone. My friend Orm, who has saved us all today, has a different religion from mine and my wife's and yet we are blood brothers. Can we not be friends with you, as well?"

He held out his hand, and after a moment Gudrun took it. "Well," she said, "for my part there can be peace. I cannot answer for my people. But if you will come with me I will do what I can for you. It is no small deed your friend Orm has done today."

"I thank you. We will come," Thorgeir said, and limped to get his sword from the corner where it had been dashed.

"We will come," said Ylga, sourly, "but I will keep my bow strung."

Outside, the sleet had stopped, but the wind drove its blades through them as they stepped into the open. The sky was still overcast, a darker gray than before, oppressive and threatening. Gudrun led them away from the high escarpment where the cave mouth yawned, and some distance to the north of it began to climb a wide spine of rock that rose toward a high ridge. The others followed, bending their heads against the wind. The spine met the face of the ridge and here a ledge had been cut, ascending at an angle, just wide enough for one person to walk along provided he walked with care. Up it they went, and when they came to the top of the ridge they found themselves looking unexpectedly down into a sheltered valley filled with the spindly treelike stalks. Among the bristling branches were the roofs of huts, made of thin slabs of gray stone.

A zigzag track, partly the natural separation of the rock, partly the work of hands, descended into the valley, a long but not too arduous climb. As Gudrun and the others reached the bottom, people began gathering, looking curiously at the newcomers. They were most of them dark haired, with proud but serious faces, self-contained and quiet, speaking in low voices, even the children unusually silent. It was as if they did not want their voices to echo among the rocks which surrounded them. They were dressed in leather, or in curious short-haired furs the color of wood smoke, and many wore gray cloaks with hoods, like Gudrun's. They kept their distance, and Thorgeir felt something almost eerie in their restraint.

To distract himself from the quiet and the staring eyes, he looked about the village. The houses were made of stone, thick-walled and huddled closely together. There were no gardens, as there were in the lands he knew, no sign of selva, no greenery at all, but in clearings here and there large patches of a rusty brown moss interspersed with low, thick-fleshed creamy funguses. He wondered whether they were cultivated.

Gudrun stopped, at last, before a building larger than the others but very low, too low it seemed for anyone to stand upright in it. But when they went round to the door, Thorgeir saw that it was reached by a ramp going down to it, and understood that the place was dug into the ground. He guessed that it must be a Moot hall, for it was large enough to hold perhaps a hundred people, and a moment later Gudrun, turning to face the crowd, said, "Let us all go inside, for I have something important to tell you."

When she opened the door, a musty, damp, earth smell wafted out. As they entered, the amber glow of crystals appeared, only a few clusters set among the stones of the walls.

Gudrun stepped aside, pulling the other three with her, and the people came down the ramp and pressed inside, sitting cross-legged on the floor, rustling and whispering. When they were all in, Gudrun shut the door and held up her hand. The crystals she had brought from the cave were brighter than the others, perhaps because she was holding them, and the light shone yellow through the flesh of her fingers.

"The Hryllir is dead!" she cried.

That news released them; the uncanny silence broke, and low voices called and exclaimed, seeming, after the stillness, as loud as shouts.

A man rose, bent and stooped with age, leaning upon a stick. In the dimness his face could not be made out, only shadowy holes for his deep-set eyes, a white beard and long white hair hanging to his shoulders.

"This is a wonder you tell us, Gudrun," said he, in a husky voice. "I see that you bring three strangers with you, and I guess there is a tale worth telling. But let us bring more light that we may see their faces."

Gudrun waited while people ran out of the hall and returned with rough lamps, a dozen crude pots filled with oil in which floated wicks. These were set on the floor in front of Thorgeir and his companions so that a smoky light was cast on them.

Gudrun said, "I was hunting stokkna near Ovinirmegin when, from the height, I saw these three coming up from the south. I watched them and saw the woman slay the ovinur with an arrow, shooting into its open mouth."

Whispers went round the hall. "Yes," she continued, "it was a great feat, and so I did not attempt to waylay them but was content to follow them. They crossed by Sudur col and climbed up on the mountain. Then it began to sleet, and they took refuge in the Hryllir's cave. I saw them face the Hryllir. That man was struck down by it, and this man stabbed it with a forked stick and slew it."

She touched Orm on the chest. "Orm Handskill is his name, and skillful is his hand. Now the cave is open to us and there are crystals enough for the whole village. Say, did I do well to leave the strangers unharmed?"

A murmur arose, and the old man said, heavily, "Good may come of evil, yet how can we excuse evil? You have done well, daughter of Hallr, but you have broken the law and must be punished for it. As for these three, before we judge them let us hear why they came into our land. For if they came as far as the cave of the Hryllir, it was not merely to hunt the stokkna."

Thorgeir stepped forward. He squinted into the dimness, wondering how much he could say. It would have been hard enough to make his own folk believe him, but how could he persuade these people, hostile to strangers as they were, of the truth of his quest? Had they ever heard of Budri, or of the ylvan? He remembered the words of Ragn the Peacemaker, when speaking of Frodi's plans: "A smaller group would listen to reason where a larger one might be pulled in too many ways." He decided to speak as frankly as he could but to say as little as possible.

He said, "I and my friends come from the far south. We knew nothing of you until we met Gudrun Hallr's-daughter, and we thought all this land was empty of humankind. Our country is faced by a great danger, and an obligation was put upon us three to go forth and find the temple of Arveid and ask the goddess for Her help. Our ancient tales say that some-where far in the north that temple lies. It may be that we will perish on the way, but we must do what we have vowed to do.

"I swear to you by my honor that we mean no harm here. All that we ask is shelter for the night, and food and drink, for we have had nothing since last night. If you will not let us stay, then let us leave in peace and find our fate elsewhere."

The villagers had listened in a silence so attentive as to be uncanny. When Thorgeir had finished, they stirred and he heard them whispering.

A voice said, "They are mad."

The old man struck the ground with his staff and they were still again.

"You have heard," he said. "Now speak, all those who will."

From the shadows of the meetinghouse, someone said, "It is as we have always said, the people in the warm lands are madmen. We cannot slay them for their madness. Let them go away."

Another, deeper voice, said, "If indeed one of them has slain the Hryllir, they have given us a gift hard to repay."

"The law is the law," a third voice put in. "Shall we receive outlanders and heathen? Would they receive one of us? Nor did they mean to make us a gift."

"The law is our servant, not our master," said another, this one a sweet, silvery voice. "It is we who make it, and we who can amend it. For my part, I will be glad of light and warmth whether it was meant as a gift or not. I believe the young man, for he speaks openly and honestly, not expecting to be believed. I think, however, that he and his friends will not live long, for there is no temple of his goddess in this land."

"Let us vote on the matter," said the deep voice. "But let Einarr speak last, as is his right."

The old man said, "I, too, believe them. If the vote goes for them, I will offer them my own house. It is clear that they are wanderers and not warriors coming against us, and so they are sacred to Odin who was himself a wanderer. Now, let all those who are against the guest-right speak further if they wish to."

There was a long silence, and someone at the very back of the hall said, in a fat, jolly voice, "I say, let us vote and then go as quickly as we can to get some of those crystals. The nights are growing colder."

There was some soft laughter, and the old man said, "Is it the will of the folk that the strangers be given the safety of the hearth?"

The subdued noise of dozens of fists pounding the earth floor answered him.

"So be it," said he. And more formally, turning to Thorgeir and the others, he said, "Welcome be the guest to hall and hearth. Rest beneath our roof as if it were your own."

The words spanned distance and time, and brought tears to Thorgeir's eyes, for they reminded him of Hjal Broadbiter.

Gudrun said, "I know that they are hungry—"

"Let the meeting end, then," the old man said. "They are welcome in my house."

Somewhat later, Orm sat back with a sigh and loosened his belt. "I am alive again," he said.

They had eaten strange dishes: a nutty-tasting porridge, a thick, filling stew of some sort, heavy dark bread and for drink a clay pitcher full of milky liquid with a lively, spicy taste, very refreshing.

Thorgeir moved his stool back from the table and said to their host, the old man whose name was Einarr Helmbreaker, "Never have I eaten or drunk so well. In this bare, hard land I cannot guess how you find porridge or bread, or a drink like this."

Einarr chuckled. "From the bounty of the mountains. The porridge is made from the seed of a plant that grows south of here, where we hunt the stokkna—"

"A tall spike with fluttering white disks on it?" said Ylga.

"Just so. The stew is made from moss and the meat of the great furred lizard, the bread from fungus, and the drink is the sap we find within the needles of the hymlic tree."

"Those tall, thin, ghostly things with bristles?" said Orm.

"Yes. One has only to gather a bunch of the bristles, as you call them, and squeeze them."

"By the eye of Udi," said Orm, laughing, "we were parched with thirst and all we had to do was stretch up a hand."

" 'Need teaches the naked how to spin,' " Einarr said. A shadow passed over his wrinkled face. "Hard has it been for us in this land, where the selva cannot grow nor cattle graze."

Thorgeir glanced at Gudrun, who sat beside Einarr, who was her foster father. "Gudrun hinted something to us of your history," he said. "She told us that people in the south had driven you out of your own place."

"You know nothing of it?" asked Einarr.

Thorgeir shook his head.

"We are of the Old Religion."

"What is that?" said Ylga.

Einarr sighed. "Are we so utterly forgotten? Have you never heard of Ragnarok, the End of the World?" And in his creaking, hoarse voice, he chanted,

> *An axe-age, a sword-age   shields shall be cloven;*
> *A wind age, a wolf age   ere the world totters.*

"Every child knows that," said Thorgeir. "But—"

"We believe that it has already happened," said Einarr. "The last great battle took place long ago, when the world perished. The Wolf swallowed the sun; he whom you call Udi but whom we still call by his old name, Odin, fell there and all the Aesir with him, and his enemies as well. It was the end of all things. But do you not know the tale of what was to come afterward? 'A new earth shall come forth from the water, greener than before, and the sun shall bear a daughter fairer than herself.' That daughter was Arveid, the Golden Sun. She dwells in the west, where She lies down to sleep every night, and it was She who gave mankind the gift of the selva."

He paused, and drank to clear his throat, while they stared at him, spellbound. He went on, "Not all men believed as we did, for the world was full of heresy and error, but still we lived at peace with our neighbors. Then, many long years ago, in the town of Haegri, there sprang up the teaching that Arveid was a mortal woman. It was spread about by a man named Bjarni Tyrna's-son, and so stubborn and hard of heart was he that he could not abide anyone who thought otherwise from himself. Many were put to death who would not accept the new belief, and we, although we lived far up in Breitadal, were especially persecuted. In the end, there was a great manslaying and those of us who were left fled away northward to take refuge here. Sun-Arveid helped us, and brought us to this valley where we learned to survive. But now, our law is that none of us should give help or friendship to the Hateful Ones from the south under pain of punishment, except by the will of all the folk."

When he had done, Thorgeir said, speaking as if dazed, "This is all strange, more than strange. For we are following in the footsteps of a legend, and we have come east of the sun and west of the moon to do as Budri Brightface did, and now you tell us that Ragnarok has been fought and long ago finished. I feel more than ever like one in a dream."

Einarr drew his brows together. "Budri Brightface?" he said, slowly. "The ancient saga of the killing of the monster from the water?"

"You know that tale, then?" said Thorgeir.

Einarr nodded. "Every child knows it. But how can you do as Budri did?"

"We do not know how we can," Ylga burst out. "We must! For the kraken is coming again. Tell them, Thorgeir."

Thorgeir told his story again, from beginning to end. When he had done, Einarr said, "That, then, was your mission and the danger you spoke of. I can see why you did not tell it all to our Moot."

"But can such a thing be believed?" said Gudrun. "A vision of the night, a beast that speaks, a myth returning?"

"We have come all this way because we believe it," Ylga said, sharply.

"And I believe it," said Einarr, somberly. "I have lived long enough to know that truth has many faces. Would these three have believed that such a creature as the Hryllir could exist? This tale has much in it that I do not understand, but I believe that it can be so. And if it is so, and the kraken is as you describe it, we, too, are doomed. If it sucks up all the moisture in living things, then it will devour the hymlic trees, for there is water in their sap."

"Ah!" Gudrun exclaimed. "I never thought of that."

"As for the temple of Arveid," mused Einarr, almost to himself, "our own history speaks of it, for it is said that Bjarni Tyrna's-son found it. The sight of the goddess drove him mad, so that when he returned to his own land he preached the foul heresy that she was only a mortal woman, because his brains were disturbed. So the temple must be there, somewhere. What says the Saga of Budri?"

Ylga said, as if once again she had the children before her, 'Budri armed himself and set out. He went to the land east of the sun and west of the moon, the land beyond the north wind where the ground is frozen night and day, and nothing grows. There is nothing but rock there, as red as blood. There, beside a lake of black ice, he found the Tree Illthorn which bears neither fruit nor leaf, and between two of its roots lay the temple of Arveid."

"Just so," said Einarr. "We, too, call those mountains the Wife of Glenr and the Mirror of Gefjun, the sun and the moon. What is more, I know that there is a land where the ground is frozen night and day, and there is nothing but rock as red as blood, for I have seen it with my own eyes."

Thorgeir stiffened. "What?" he said. "Where is it?"

"North by west," Einarr replied. "I was young, then. Do you know how many winters I have weathered? Eighty-two. And this was sixty years ago and more."

He rubbed his eyes with a knotty finger. "A long time, eh? I was your age, and drawn by adventure. I was sick of this valley and these mountains, and I took my weapons and set out to see what lay still further north—'beyond the north wind,' as the saga says.

"Five days I journeyed, eating and drinking sparingly, for by the third day the hymlic trees had vanished, there was little rock moss and nothing much to hunt. It was cold, there, as cold as the Fimbel-winter, the last terrible winter that foretold Ragnarok, but at last I climbed down through a gorge, half a day's climb, and came out upon a wide plain. The ground was partly covered with some low, creeping plant but it was all frozen, stems and leaves, and beneath it the earth was frozen hard. And here and there lay rocks in the shape of tree trunks and they were red. Just so," he said, "as red as heart's blood.

"I went on a short way, and then my courage began to ebb, for I had almost no food left and my water bottles were nearly empty. So I turned back. But although it is sixty years, I can still tell you the road."

Thorgeir sat deep in thought, his chin on his fist, and then he said, "The rocks were shaped like tree trunks, you say?"

Einarr nodded. "Some were like pieces of fallen trees, and some like stumps, but all as if turned to stone by wizardry."

"Then perhaps Illthorn, too, is there—a tree without fruit or leaf!" He stood up, his face shining. "That way lies our path."

Orm raised his eyebrows. "Tonight?" he said, with such a look of comical concern that they all laughed.

Not that night, nor indeed the next day did they go, for in the morning many of the Hill Folk came to meet Thorgeir and his companions. For all their hatred of strangers, once they had given the guest-right they were kindly and hospitable. Then the full tale of the quest was told, and Einarr's word carried great weight, for he was not only the oldest of them but greatly respected for his measured thought. He recalled to them that Bjarni Tyrna's-son had found the temple—from which finding had come their exile—and told them of his own journey to the place of red rocks. They were impressed by the way in which many of the words of the saga of Budri were shown to be true. If some of them still thought Thorgeir and his companions were insane, they said nothing, for they were a people much given to keeping things to themselves. Some of them remained to discuss the matter in their slow, quiet way.

A gray-haired woman with a hard, lined face, whose musical voice they recognized from the meeting the night before, said, "You will never reach your goal—if it exists at all—without preparation, for if what Einarr says of the road is true, you will starve or freeze before crossing that red waste. We must fit you out with heavy cloaks and provide you with food and drink, but even more to the point we must give you some of the crystals, for with them you will be able to endure the bitter cold. This morning, people are going to fetch a supply from the cave."

This seemed wise, and Thorgeir agreed in spite of his desire for haste. He could not keep his thoughts from what might be happening at home, and often talked of it with Ylga. Had it come to war, or had Ragn and Bera been able to restrain Svip and his followers? And with what power was Athils securing himself? The thought of Athils filled Thorgeir with sorrow, for they had once been close and Thorgeir had looked up to his elder brother as a bold and noble warrior. Yet it had been Athils' doing that their father now sat in the silent dark, buried in a howe among the other dead with his sword across his knees. And from those thoughts, Thorgeir's mind ranged to some unknown place—how far, or in what direction he did not know, for the ylvan had not told him—where the kraken prepared for its flight and from which it would come, or was perhaps already flapping on its deadly way searching for food and drawing closer to the habitations of humankind.

That day, he and Orm and Ylga went over their gear. The villagers came forward with gifts of new clothes, leather tunics and leggings and shoes with thick, soft soles most suitable for rock climbing. Orm was given a knapsack and a hunting knife by Gudrun, her father's, she said. They were also given new sleeping-cloths and gray cloaks with hoods, light in weight but warm and waterproof, made of fibers stripped from the skin of the hymlic tree—for it was too thin to be called bark—beaten and woven like cloth. The saplings of the hymlic, when dried and seasoned, were used by the people as rafters and poles, for they were almost as tough as the wood of the aska, although useless for fuel, for they only smoked and smoldered. Orm chose two from a pile behind Einarr's house, and he and Thorgeir had a good hour's exercise, going at each other hammer and tongs to the delight of a ring of children and even some adults.

Gudrun watched, too, and later when they sat on the ground mopping their sweaty faces and recovering their breath, she said, "It will long be told among us how with a stick no better than that the Hryllir was vanished. It was a wonder, when swords were of no avail."

"The thing had some power over metal, that is clear," said Thorgeir. "Are there any more of the creatures?"

Gudrun shook her head. "Our history says that that one was here when first we settled in this valley. Some said it was a creature of Surtr, the Enemy of the Gods, but this was held to be blasphemy, since Surtr perished in the Last Battle." She paused, and then went on, "But you believe none of that, neither that the battle of Ragnarok has been fought nor that the world was remade. What is it you believe?"

Thorgeir pondered. Raising his face to hers, he said, "Does it matter? Whatever I may believe—or Ylga, or Orm—we have nothing but good will for you and your folk. Is there not room in the wide world for all of us? The best man and woman I ever knew, save my own parents, were of a different religion from mine. I know they judged each person by his deeds. Yes," he added, sadly, "and died for it."

Gudrun shook her head. "It is strange to me. We have lived so long hating and knowing we were hated that I cannot think otherwise."

Orm said, "Einarr told us that your goddess is the Golden Sun. Does not the sun shine on every land alike?"

Gudrun sighed. Without another word, she got to her feet

and walked slowly away toward the house, her eyes on the ground.

The next morning, the three companions prepared to leave. The village had one very deep well, which had found a trickle of water in the heart of the rock, and from this slender source their water bottles were filled. They were also given three leather canteens of hymlic juice, and a good store of bread, smoked meat, dried moss, and mushrooms. A large quantity of the crystals had been brought from the cave, although most had been left where they were since when they were not dislodged their power seemed to last endlessly; half a dozen large clusters were carefully packed in leather and stowed in the knapsacks. Then they sat down with Einarr for the last time, to go over the map he had drawn them.

"A five-day journey," said Thorgeir. "Perhaps we can do it in four, since we shall have neither to hunt nor to find our way. Farewell, Einarr. Maybe we will meet again."

"You will be welcome here whenever you come," said Einarr.

Gudrun entered, throwing back the hood of her cloak. "You are ready to leave?" she said.

"We are. Nor will we forget you," said Thorgeir. "I only hope that your bringing us here has caused you no more trouble."

"I have been judged," Gudrun said, quietly. "Yet my breaking of the law was held to be good as well as ill, and so my punishment is light. The council has allowed me to choose it for myself."

"What have you chosen?" Orm asked. "Do not be too hard on yourself."

She turned her brilliant gaze upon him. "I have chosen to go into exile," she replied. "And if you three will have me, to go with you and help you on your quest."

Einarr uttered a long sigh. "I feared as much," said he.

She went to the old man's side and, stooping, kissed him. "Do not grieve for me, foster father. I have long owed a debt of vengeance for my father's death, and now I will repay it. And I must try their way—to stand beside them in such a venture although they are unbelievers."

She looked at Ylga. "You have not liked me from the first, for you thought I put your man in danger. Will you have me go with you?"

Ylga smiled, and held out both her hands.

VII

IN ARVEID'S HEART

RED rock, low red vegetation as hard as the rock, red earth that rang underfoot. It was as if that last terrible combat which the Hill Folk believed had ended the world had been fought on this plain and had stained the land forever. The four travelers looked across it aghast. Even the nooning sun seemed smaller, more darkly orange, and without warmth.

They had been four days on the way, long days of hard, steady going, of short rests, of careful rationing of their food so that they were always a little hungry and thirsty, always a little weary. Yet they had done as Thorgeir had hoped and had beaten Einarr's time. That morning, they had climbed down a long gorge, a steep, tiring descent among tumbled, sharp-edged boulders, and now the blood-colored waste spread out before them.

Its flatness and featurelessness made their hearts sink, for it seemed to go on interminably. It was strewn with rocks which, just as Einarr had said, resembled sections of tree trunks, cylindrical and with markings like bark on their surfaces. But they were like trees which had fallen and shattered; the largest of them was no higher than the height of a tall man. There was no wind, for which they were thankful since there was no shelter, but the air was so biting that it froze the moisture in their nostrils, and the very tears it brought to their eyes frosted their lashes. Every night of the journey they had been grateful for the crystals which allowed them to sleep warm; now, they were even more thankful, and each of them held a cluster close as they looked about.

Gudrun stooped and touched one of the plants which crept along the ground. Its thick stem was covered with thick, round leaves, so closely packed they seemed like scales.

"It is as cold as ice," she said.

She held her crystals close to it. Steam burst forth and the leaves shriveled and collapsed; a thin crimson liquid ran down, forming a pool which coagulated before their eyes and began to freeze.

Gudrun shuddered. "Even the plants bleed. It is a place of death."

Orm put his arm around her waist and drew her close, but said nothing.

Ylga, shading her eyes, surveyed the horizon. "There, somewhat to the west," she said. "Look, Thorgeir. Can you not see faint shadows?"

He peered, squinting under his hand. At last, he said, "Too slender to be mountains. They rise straight up, almost like—"

He left the sentence hanging, and she finished it for him. "—like leafless trees?"

They stared at each other, and he said, "I do not know. But let us try that way."

On open ground they could run again, although they had to avoid the plants which were too hard to tread upon. They trotted in line, Thorgeir picking the way. The cold air was like knives in their throats, but their bodies grew warmer; they put their crystals in their knapsacks, and soon they were almost too warm. On and on, while the sun declined, and the faint shapes on the horizon seemed to grow no nearer. At dusk, they spread two of their sleeping-cloths on the ground and draped the other two over their hooded heads, like little tents, and in this shelter with their crystals in the center as a campfire, they were snug enough for their dinner. They slept close together, huddled about the crystals which kept life in them in the fearsome cold. In the morning, when they broke camp, there was a damp patch beneath the sleeping-cloths where the earth had softened, but in the few moments it took them to pack their knapsacks it was threaded with ice.

All that day they trotted, but with more hope, for by mid-afternoon the shapes were plain to see, although hard to understand for they were like nothing any of them had ever seen before. Huge columns of stone, they seemed, as high as hills, large enough in girth to cover a village, sheer sided, nearly as wide at the tops as at the bottoms. They were all of a dark brownish-red, and their resemblance to a grove of tree trunks was striking, but they were trees without branches or tops.

"If anywhere," said Orm, "there is where we should find Illthorn."

They ran on for another hour or two, until the sun was low and the immensely long shadows of the stone columns fell for miles across the plain. As they drew closer to them, the rocks lying about became larger, huge drums and barrels shot through their centers with veins of green and black shaped like the rings of wood, their outer surfaces a more brilliant scarlet. They were like fallen branches, or like smaller trees that had toppled at the feet of the larger ones. And the larger ones themselves, the great columns, could now be seen to be ridged and furrowed with patterns of bark just as the broken pieces were, with bark that had turned to stone. But it was impossible, still, to imagine trees as large as these.

They camped at the base of one. Orm ran his palm along the stone, and picked up a fragment from the ground.

"I will take oath on it, this was once wood," he said. "How could it have turned to stone?"

Gudrun said, "In the time of Ragnarok. Surely, now you must believe the truth? For clearly, this plain was the Field of Vigridr, and here the Last Battle took place. Now you must see that we are right! Here, the Aesir fell, one by one, and with them their foes, Surtr, and Garm and the Wolf Fenris. Here, so it is written, Surtr cast fire over the whole world and burned it, and here the sun was eaten and the stars fell from the heavens. In such a time, in such a place, why should not the very trees have turned to stone?"

Orm looked thoughtfully at her. "I am no great hand at belief," he said, "and I gave no more thought to your Old Religion than I did to my own. But that was before I saw this place. Now, I am not so sure. In any case," he added, with a shrug, "what does it matter? We are little likely to return with the news."

Ylga had been looking in her pack. She said, "Thorgeir, how much meat have you left? There is almost no more bread. Gudrun, see how much food you have in your knapsack. And Orm, thaw the canteens so that we can see what is left to drink."

When they had done as she asked, she shook her head. "It is as I feared. There is enough for one more day, if we tighten our belts. Let us pray to Arveid to help us, for if we do not find Her temple tomorrow, we are lost."

"Yes," Orm said, "but which Arveid? We are three different religions here. But then, perhaps one of us will reach Her."

"Orm do not joke," Gudrun said, in reproof. "We are not all so light-minded as you."

"I think," said Thorgeir, "that the Maiden sees us and hears us. If it is Her will that we find Her, we will do so. If not, no prayers will save us, and in such case perhaps it is better to meet what comes with a laugh, like Orm."

Yet in spite of his words, his dreams were full of foreboding, and when he awoke in the deep night Ylga was whimpering in her sleep. He clasped her more tightly, patting her as if she were a child, and after a time he fell asleep again, dreaming of flames, smoke and bloodshed as if this were indeed haunted ground.

Before sunrise, they were all four up and about, for none of them had slept well. In the red flush of dawn they ate a meager breakfast and then walked around the colossal trunk beside which they had camped. There were some dozens of the mighty columns, with half a mile or more between each, forming a grove of breathtaking size. About their bases, the ground was clear of the frozen vegetation but piled with more of the large rocks which they were now certain were pieces of boughs. Among these, they made their way, mile after mile, like beetles toiling among pebbles.

The sun rose higher behind them, and suddenly Thorgeir saw, half a mile away behind one of the columns, a silvery wink. He stopped, and at the same time, Orm said in a choked voice, "Illthorn!"

Thorgeir gazed one way, then another; Orm caught hold of his shoulder and pointed high up with his staff to that same trunk near which the glint of silver showed. It had kept part of one of its boughs, curving grandly upward and outward to the splintered end, large enough on its upper side for a house to be built on it. The bough gave it more the look of a tree than any of its neighbors.

Thorgeir drew in a breath of wonder. "Yes," he said, "and there is something at the bottom."

"I see it," said Ylga. "A silver dome, I think."

They began to walk toward it, but with growing reluctance. At a distance, dwarfed by the giant tree, it had looked small; as they drew nearer to it, it lifted above them, a vast, dully shining curve of metal. They moved more slowly, going a few steps, pausing, going on again, awe mounting within them.

That it was a building of some sort they could not doubt, but utterly foreign to all they knew. They could not conceive how it had been hammered out of steel, or silver, nor what hands might have made it, but there was no doubt in any of their minds that they looked upon the temple of the Goddess. It lay in an open space that was black and smooth and shining like ice. It was windowless, pitted from great age, and decorated with many curious projections, arrangements of rods and plates and tubes. It was in the shape of a cylinder, lying on its side, one end bluntly pointed, the other flattened, and near the pointed end there was a wide door with neither hinge nor handle, closed, but with a ramp leading up to it from the ground.

They came still closer. And there, plainly to be seen, was the proof of their finding: a little way to the left of the door, in large old-fashioned runes still to be found in some book-scrolls, was the word ARVEID. Below it was a square of dark blue on which was a red cross edged with white.

They stared in silence. Then Gudrun slowly sank down upon her knees.

"It is the Sun-cross," she murmured. "The sign of the Daughter of Glenr."

"It is the *en* rune," Orm said, hoarsely.

"All the tales are true," said Ylga. "Golden Maiden, protect us." And she, too, knelt beside Gudrun.

Shivers ran up Thorgeir's spine and the hair rose on his neck. He was filled with wonder, with a joy bordering on panic terror; his heart beat so that he was near fainting. Elation at his success combined with the presence of the Goddess to overwhelm him.

But not altogether. The spirit and determination which had driven him so far and made the others follow him, upheld him.

"Let us enter," he said.

"No," said Orm.

Thorgeir stared at his friend. *"You,* Orm—are you afraid?"

"No," Orm answered. "I am full of amazement, but I am not afraid. But this is for you, Thorgeir. Yours was the decision to undertake the quest. It was for you the spaeman wrote the stave:

> *There must he walk   the weapon wielder,*
> *In Arveid's heart   let hero seek.*

"You alone led us here, knowing from the beginning that only one hand can hold whatever weapon is the Goddess's gift. Yours alone must be the honor of going before Her. Or do you not agree?"

"He is right," said Ylga, rising. The tears brimmed in her eyes and ran down her cheeks. "I wish it were not so."

Thorgeir bowed his head. He had in truth known from the first that this was his destiny, and looking within himself he knew that he welcomed it even as he dreaded it. He went to Ylga and clasped her in his arms. He kissed her tenderly, her wet cheeks, her trembling lips. He let her go, bent to kiss Gudrun, and embraced Orm. Then he turned away and strode resolutely, still without a word, toward the temple.

As he set foot on the ramp, the door moved, first inward, then to one side, with a humming vibration that made the ramp tremble slightly. Within, all was dark. He climbed boldly. As he reached the doorway, lights appeared inside, a soft but sunny radiance, showing a passage with walls of a warm, pleasing yellow like the flower of the kala bean. He looked back at his three companions. Ylga raised her hand. He set his face to the front and stepped firmly inside. The door closed behind him.

He had expected some great hall, but instead there was only the passage, wide enough for six to stand abreast, running a short distance straight before him and joining another, narrower corridor, that one pale blue. There were incomprehensible symbols marked on the walls, and at intervals round devices, like the bosses of shields, made of shining crystal or metal. He hesitated, unsure what to do, and at last walked forward to the cross passage. All at once, a faint chiming of a bell was heard, three strokes.

A voice spoke from the air. "Welcome. Please follow these directions. Turn to the left, pass three corridors, turn right into the fourth and proceed until you come to the Information Center."

Its accent was strange, but understandable. There was no doubt it was the voice of a woman.

His hands were damp. He drew a deep breath and went on, to the left, following the directions he had been given. He touched one of the walls as he passed, and it was very smooth, but he could not tell what it was made of. It was cool, but not as icy as the rocks outside, and then for the first time he realized that the air was mild, not warm except by contrast with the outer world, but comfortable enough so that he could put back his cloak and undo the neckstring of his tunic. His hand brushed the amulet that hung round his neck and for an instant he closed his fingers around it with a shiver. It had come from this place; it was returning home.

He turned right into the fourth corridor. He had noticed, at intervals, closed doors as he had gone along, but now there were open doors and peeping inside one he saw a room on the walls of which were painted children in unfamiliar garments at play, another in which were strange chairs of some puffy material and tables of metal, another in which there seemed to be only cushions on the floor and racks of little boxes, hundreds of them. At last, he came to a larger door at the end of the corridor, and as he approached, it slid aside for him as the outer door had done.

He entered a large hall in which everything was so totally outside his experience that, except for curving rows of seats, he did not know what he was looking at. His eye saw distorted pieces of steel, squares of color, large boxes with windows in them within which disks jerkily moved, rows of buttons, shapes that might be made of metal or enamel decorated with small blinking stars. With a fierce effort of the will he kept himself upright, clenching one hand upon the pommel of his sword, the other upon his belt.

In a ringing voice, he said, "Maiden, I am here."

He waited for some appearance, but nothing changed. Then, at last, from one end of the hall the voice he had heard before, the voice of the Goddess, said, "Who are you?"

"I am Thorgeir Frodi's-son, called Red Thorgeir," said he.

"Where do you come from, Thorgeir Frodi's-son?" said the voice.

"From Velir in Vollingsland."

"Ah, yes," said the voice. "I know that place. Coordinates A2446—S2910. One moment . . . Budri Thorkil's-son came from there. Is that name familiar to you?"

"Budri Brightface," said Thorgeir, in a shaking voice.

"I have no record of that name."

"It was so he was called after he slew the kraken." And gathering boldness, Thorgeir went on, "You helped him to that deed. And now I have followed him to tell you that your people are in danger once more, for the kraken is coming upon us. Help us, Arveid! If you account me worthy, give me weapons and let me go to face the beast as Budri once did."

There was stillness. Then the voice said, "Thorgeir Frodi's-son, you shall have what you ask for. In this place, you may ask whatever you will and I must answer. But I am not Arveid. Arveid has been dead for twelve hundred years.''

Thorgeir began to tremble, so that he had to catch the back of one of the seats to steady himself. He sat down, and the chair yielded luxuriously beneath him. He looked at the end of the room from whence the voice came but saw only incomprehensible forms, twinkling lights as of a night sky, gleaming metal, patches of blue or yellow, red or green.

He said, ''Then Bjarni Tyrna's-son was right. The unbelievers are right. Arveid was a mortal woman.''

''No,'' said the voice. ''Professor Morten Arveid was a theoretical physicist.''

Thorgeir heard the words, but he understood them no more than he understood what the forms and devices were that he was looking at.

''I do not know what you mean,'' he said, at last. ''I do not know the meaning of any of it. Forgive me.''

There was another silence. The voice said, with careful patience, ''Professor Arveid was a man. He invented a way of moving things through the heavens, from one world to another. When it became impossible to live on earth any longer, many ships were built, like this one, which carried the people to other places where they could go on living.''

Thorgeir rubbed his face hard, in bewilderment. He seized upon one of the things that seemed to make sense. ''Do you tell me,'' he said, ''that the Old Religion is right and that the Last Battle has been fought? The world has ended?''

''The world has ended,'' said the voice, ''but not in battle.

In filth. The land, the water, the air, all became foul so that nothing could grow, the rivers were tainted, and every breath that was drawn was bitter. The sea itself was filled with poison.''

''How—?'' Thorgeir began.

''It was the greed and folly of humankind,'' said the voice, speaking calmly and gently as ever. ''If you pile dung high will it not kill the grass beneath? The day came when the earth died. In many lands, in thousands of places, the ships were prepared, using Professor Arveid's devices, and fled away to find other worlds.

''This ship came from a northern land called Iceland, and it carried the ancestors of your people, all of you. It was named in honor of Professor Arveid; you saw his name upon its hull.''

Thorgeir sat with closed eyes, trying to absorb what he had heard, although his brain was whirling. He heard the voice still speaking, but many of its words were empty for him.

''It was a terrible struggle for those settlers. This world had a lesser gravity than their own, which they had to adapt to. There was less water and the problem of food was great, but on their own world botanists had developed a plant which was the salvation of many of the refugees, including those who came here. And so, in time, they survived. Perhaps only Icelanders could have done so here. They learned to live upon this earth as their ancestors had first done in their own harsh, stony, native land.

"Luckily, there were few hostile beasts. The ovinur, the stinging lizard, the red asp—and, once, the kraken."

He lifted his head at that. "The kraken," he said. "Tell me of the kraken."

"It is not one creature, but many. They live in the waters of a lake, far to the northeast of Vollingsland. Over hundreds of years they grow, and as the water shrinks they draw together, first in clumps, eventually into what seems a single beast. Then, scattering their seed, which will grow again when the lake rises once more, they fly searching for water. They suck the moisture from everything they find, moving ever southward, and in time they come to the sea and there, in the salt waves, they die at last."

Thorgeir clasped his hands together so tightly that the pain made him wince. "Udi!" he said. "It is long since I was told by the ylvan that the kraken was coming. Where is it now? Has it come to Velir? Am I too late?"

"Wait," said the voice. "Let me see."

After a short time, during which Thorgeir sat numbly trying to grasp all that he had heard, it said, "You are not too late, but there is little time to lose. The kraken is moving toward the place you call Nimma's Field."

Thorgeir sprang to his feet: "Do not fear," the voice said calmly. "I will give you the weapons I gave Budri Thorkil's-son, and you must be taught how to use them."

"The distance—"

"Will not matter. But all rests on you. Are you courageous, Thorgeir, and quick to learn?"

"I will try."

"Have you no more questions?"

He stood, chin on breast, in thought. "You tell me, then, that the Goddess Arveid never existed," he said. "That her name was that of some learned man, and that our own people made the selva. And so, we have all been living in ignorance and folly all these years. Why did not Budri tell the truth? Why did Bjarni return with some wild tale that Arveid was a mortal woman?"

"I cannot answer that," said the voice. "Perhaps you will answer it yourself, one day."

He sighed. "And you?" he said. "Who are you?"

"I am the Guardian. I was left here by your ancestors, those first settlers, to give what protection and advice could be given to their descendants."

"Let me see your face," said Thorgeir.

"You have been looking at me all this time," said the voice of the machine on the platform.

VIII

ON NIMMA'S FIELD

THE small, bloody sun sank; the west flamed and darkened, and still Ylga, Orm and Gudrun waited. They ate the last crumbs they could find in their knapsacks, drank the last mouthfuls of water. In this cold air, the stars blazed, the Ale Horn far down upon the horizon.

"Shall we ever see him again?" said Gudrun. "Or has Arveid taken him away?"

"He will return, I am sure of it," Ylga said staunchly, but within her, her spirit quailed.

They covered themselves with the sleeping-cloths and slept at last. And with the first bright rays of morning, as they sat up hungry and fearful, the wide door of the temple slid aside.

Ylga sprang eagerly to her feet. But at the figure that appeared, she shrank back, and behind her Orm's breath hissed between his teeth.

It was Thorgeir who stood there, for they could see his

face, but he was changed. Grim and sad he appeared, already clothed in a terrible remoteness. His head was covered by a helmet of some transparent material, crested with twisted strands of metal, with round metal pieces at the cheeks and a gray collar that held it on his shoulders. On his back was what they at first took to be a shield, but then saw was a double tube of metal held by a harness. About his waist was a heavy belt with a pair of boxes attached to it, and in his hand he held a wand of steel, hilted like a sword, shining in the morning sun.

He regarded his friends through the clear visor of the helm, and his eyes were somber. He gave them no greeting, but said, "I must go, and at once. But there is food and shelter in the—in the temple."

He began to descend the ramp, moving slowly, and they drew away from him. He was no longer their friend; he had, in their eyes, already become one with Budri Brightface.

But Ylga, as she stepped back, held out her hands and sobbed, and in a faint, heartbroken voice said, "Thorgeir, farewell."

His face softened. "Ylga," he said, "I cannot embrace you now, armed as I am. And I have seen and heard too much."

Orm said, "You tell us there is food within the temple, but—dare we go inside?"

Thorgeir hesitated. There was no way in which he could explain what he had seen, and they would find out for themselves in any case, as he had done. He could not guess how it might change them.

He said, "You have no choice if you are not to starve. Afterward—wait for me, if you can, for if I live I must return these arms to the temple." He looked at them across the gulf of his knowledge, his eyes lingering on Ylga, and then said, "Farewell."

For a good part of the night, he had learned the uses of the three things the Guardian had given him. She—for although he knew now it was not human, he still thought of it as a woman, just as his ancestors had called their ship "she," thus taking the first steps toward making Arveid feminine— she had given them strange names which he could not remember, but for him they were the arms told of in Budri's saga: the helm Dark-hood, the boots Long-stride, the sword Direful. He had practiced their uses in a large hall in the ship designed, he was told, for exercise and games. Now he set his left hand on the knob at his belt and pressed it.

The ground dropped away beneath his feet. Far below, he caught a glimpse of the three upturned faces, and then he had to give all his attention to mastering his dizziness and the horror of the empty space between himself and the earth. This was quite different from the short jumps he had made in the exercise hall, but he calmed himself and set his mind on the flight. It was not really difficult, for his own body controlled the direction he took, but keeping his balance and his sense of which way was *up* took an effort, and at first he could not recognize what lay below him. Very soon, however, he was able to distinguish the details of the rocky plain, and from this height he could see the blue mass of Goldcrest Mountain rearing to the southeast. He had been moving at a pace no faster than a rapid walk, but now he turned the knob carefully and tilted his body forward. The air whistled past his helmet as his speed increased, and he tried to keep his body compact and lithe, to offer as little resistance to it as possible, as he had been instructed.

That distance which he and his companions had covered in so many weary days, he now spanned in a few hours. He passed high over the cliffs and ravines where the Hill Folk lived, too rapidly to guess where their village might be. He flew between the twin peaks across whose skirts he had crept laboriously with his friends. The kraken, he had been told, was coming at a long slant from the northeast toward Vollingsland, and if he held steadily in this direction he should intercept it before it could reach the mining town of Esk.

Below him now was the many-colored stony land in which they had met the ovinur. He turned somewhat more to the east. On his right, far off, shimmered the green, pleasant vale of Breita, and ahead the rounded backs of the Boldneb range. Somewhere there, lay the Pass of Boldneb, and beyond it the hard ground slanted upward to the high, barren plateau called Nimma's Field.

He had been flying for four hours, and whether he wished it or not he had to stop. The Guardian had given him some pellets in a box, and these, she had said, would give him nourishment as well as strength and endurance. But he could not take them in the air. He swooped down, landed unsteadily, and found his legs so weak he nearly fell. He took the tablets almost fearfully, swallowing them with a mouthful of water from one of the containers on his belt. In moments, he felt more awake, more fully alive, as charged with vitality as if he were in some state even more exalted than being "breath-born." He closed the visor of the helm and rose into the air once more.

The ground sped beneath him, foothills, low mountains, bare rocks, occasional dots and blurs of greenery. And then he saw on the far horizon to his left what seemed to be a dark smear across the sky. It was no more than a vague blot and yet something within him told him it was the kraken.

He glanced down to see where he was. There were dots scattered ahead upon the plain which, as he touched the knob and slackened his pace, resolved themselves into running men. He flew in a wide curve; there, near the shadow of the steep cliffs of Nimma's Edge he saw a dozen huts, dark cubes like dice cast at random, and all around them struggling fig-ures, half obscured by dust, and in the dust cloud the glint of blades.

He swept down upon them. Ten feet above them he flew, circling, and to attract their attention he touched another stud on his belt, that which set the magic working in his helm. A glowing nimbus spread about him, rainbow colored and crackling faintly.

To the warriors so desperately engaged, he appeared as a terrifying vision, a winged being flaming in the sky. As first one, then another, drew back from the fight, pointing and shouting, from that center the rings of silence went out like circles in water from a dropped stone. The clatter of blades ceased, the dust settled, and soon over the whole field there was a hush. Into it, Thorgeir sank, and as he set foot on the ground, the warriors gave back from him. Others crowded up to stare over their shoulders, Vollings and Tyrnings alike, and soon he was surrounded by a dense ring of men, but none nearer than a long ten paces.

Thorgeir gazed at them. In a great voice, he cried, "Put up your weapons!"

There was a disturbance in the ring, men were pushed aside, and Athils appeared, forcing his way through. He wore a byrnie of black iron scales, an iron and leather helm covered his long brown hair, and he bore a long sword in his hand clotted with blood. He stared incredulously at his brother.

"Thorgeir," he said, "is it you? Or is it something in your shape?"

"It is I, brother, the son of Frodi." He could not help the bitterness in his voice. "Let the battle cease. The kraken is coming."

There was a shadow of uneasiness on Athils' face, but he said, boldly, "I have heard that before. A child's story to cover treachery. I do not know whence you come, or what sorcery you have been dabbling in that lets you drop from the sky, but it needs more than sorcery to cover your guilt. You think to save your friends, the Detestable People. But we told them that we knew their plan. Too late, they tried to send their forces here, to Nimma's Field, to fall upon Esk. We have them outnumbered. Not you, nor anyone, shall hold our hand until they are all slain."

And with that, before another word could be said or a move made, he raised his sword and lunged at Thorgeir's breast.

Six inches short, the sword's point stopped. There was a flash so bright it dazzled the onlookers, a whiplike crack that sent the ring of men stumbling away. Athils recoiled, as if he had been struck. He threw his arms wide, the sword flew from his hand, and he toppled backward, stone dead.

A cry burst from Thorgeir's lips. He looked down upon his brother, and said, "Not of my doing was this deed. Ah, Athils, you were ever headstrong."

Lifting his head, he glared at the stunned warriors. "You fools!" he roared. "Will you believe me now? I come from Arveid's temple. The kraken is here—go, take shelter among the rocks."

He did not watch to see what they would do, for in that instant when he looked up he had seen a dark flapping shadow like the loom of a thundercloud rise above the horizon. Touching the knob on his belt, he sprang into the air.

None of the warnings had prepared him for the size of the thing. It spread before him, as he rose to meet it, like a bank of cloud. If it had settled on the battlefield, it would have covered half the warriors. Flying toward it, he was like a gnat flying to meet a human hand.

It was not black, as it had seemed in the vision he had

had from the ylvan's mind, but the color of a sunset cloud purplish-gray against the sky. In the center it was humped like a hill, but most of its size was furnished by vast spreading membranes which beat the air with ponderous slowness. High as it was, the wind from those wings sent the dust spinning on the plain below. On the front of it, round orbs lifted on long stalks, half a dozen of them, turning their flat pupil-less gaze on Thorgeir.

He had been well schooled by the Guardian, and he was prepared when from somewhere along the front edge of the thing an aperture gaped and a shower of small globules came shooting toward him. Nevertheless, he could not help flinching as they struck his protective screen, exploding as they did so in a myriad sparkles of flame. Each one, he had been told would drain the screen of a tiny bit of its energy. It was essential for him to get above the kraken, to give whatever magic it was that fed the screen time to regain its force.

He shot upward, and just in time, for a second volley of the globules had been launched and sprayed harmlessly below him. From above, the creature lay like an island in the ocean of air. Its skin was thick and lustrous, like seaweed, dotted here and there with swollen cysts filled with a gas made by some action within it, which gave its great bulk enough lightness to remain aloft. Its eyes followed Thorgeir's flight.

"Somewhere within the hump is its nerve center," the Guardian had said, "the cluster of cells which keeps it together. You must destroy that, for no other wound will stop it."

He pointed the weapon she had given him, the metal rod set in a heavy hilt. His finger touched the stud. A thin shaft of pale blue light lanced down and struck the kraken.

It tore into the purple hide, and a gush of thin liquid, green as seawater, spouted out. Almost at once it stopped, as the skin sealed over it.

The thing flapped its wings and lurched upward suddenly, flinging at Thorgeir a thousand strands of a clear, jelly-like substance, threads of poison. They, too, winked into flame against his screen, but a few penetrated it, for Athils' death had taken more of its energy than Thorgeir knew. Thorgeir felt the caustic bite on arm and side, like bitter needles driven into his flesh.

He flew higher, desperately, turning in the air to fire his weapon again and again. Great purple-gray gobbets of its substance flaked off, green liquid dropped from it, and once more it sealed itself. Once more, it sent a swarm of globules up at Thorgeir, and when these had flared and died, the rainbow-colored aureole which had surrounded him faded and went out. His protection was gone.

He knew one more thing about the creature: it could feel nothing. Its skin was like the rind of a plant and felt no more than a tree does. Its responses were automatic and simple, it ate, it moved from place to place, it protected itself, and that was all.

He plummeted down. He landed on the back of the kraken, behind the hump of its center at the base of a tapering tail with which it steered itself. Here it could not feel him, nor could the six eyes see him, and here, for a moment, he was safe. He did not know what other defenses it might have but he would not think of anything but his task. Leveling his weapon, he pressed the stud.

The blue beam shot out like a slender sword blade, stabbing deep into the hump. Aquamarine blood spurted, spattering Thorgeir's helmet and clothing, and stinging with a nettle's fire where it touched his bare hands. Blindly, he slashed with his beam, slicing from side to side, probing ever deeper, gritting his teeth against the pain.

With a single thunderclap, the kraken burst apart. It erupted in uncountable fragments, scattering itself in a cloud of particles that darkened the sky, hurling Thorgeir away. So benumbed was he that he almost forgot he could fly. Falling dizzily, he fumbled at his belt, located the button and pushed it, soared upward again. The kraken's dust was streaming away like the ash from a volcano. In the combat, they had flown beyond Nimma's Field, and he circled back, stooping like a falcon to the battlefield, and as he went the aureole of his protective screen brightened once again about him.

So, cowering along the edge of the cliff where they had sheltered, the Tyrnings and Vollings saw him return, glittering, wet with the blood of the kraken whose destruction had stunned them.

They came, some trembling, some gape mouthed, all full of awe, to surround him, and many fell on their knees.

One said, "It is Budri Brightface come again to save us."

"No," said Thorgeir. Gazing along their ranks, he saw a

face he knew, freckled and pug nosed. "You, Hlod Erni's-son, you know me," he said.

Hlod looked at him with the eagerness of a hound. "You know my name?" he said. "Yes, you are like Thorgeir Redhair, but you have seen the Goddess. You have seen Her in Her temple. We heard a rumor, some said it was spread by Ragn the Peacemaker, that the kraken was coming and that you had gone to ask the Goddess for help, but few believed it. Forgive us for our blindness, *Herra*."

There were no titles among either Vollings or Tyrnings, where all were accounted equals, but that word—it meant "lord"—belonged to the old tales, the sagas of ancient times. As soon as Hlod had said it, the rest knelt down as if the word itself had fixed in their minds the great gulf between Thorgeir and themselves.

One of the Tyrnings, a bearded man who wore an iron necklace from which hung the golden shears of his religion, cried, "*Herra,* Slayer of the Kraken, you who have seen the face of Arveid, tell us of Her."

Thorgeir opened his mouth to reply, and paused. "There is no Goddess"—could he say that? How could he make them see what he had seen, explain what even to him was not clear?

And there was more. It had begun to dawn on him that he was no longer Thorgeir Redhair, not for these people, but Thorgeir *Herra,* Thorgeir Krakenslayer, just as that man who had once been Budri Thorkil's-son became the legend that was Budri Brightface, taking the name from this same helmet Thorgeir himself wore. He alone knew how Budri's saga ended, for the Guardian had shown him the room in the ship in which there was a little dust and a skull, all that remained of Budri who had returned the arms to the temple and had spent what remained of his life there, alone. The Guardian, being inhuman, did not know why, but Thorgeir understood it now. Budri could not go back to live again among his own people, for how can a legend rub shoulders with common folk in daily life?

One other had won his way to the temple and had returned—Bjarni Tyrna's-son. Half-crazed, perhaps, by the experience, he must have tried to tell what he had seen, and his words had been transformed into a new religion which ended in intolerance and bloodshed.

That, at least, said Thorgeir to himself, I can amend.

He became conscious of his weariness, of the pain of his blistered hands and wounded side and arm, of the weight of his helmet, the harness on his back, the belt about his waist. And of the hundreds of pairs of eyes that watched him hopefully.

He lifted himself in the air, just above their heads so that all could see him. He opened the visor of the helm so that his voice would carry more clearly.

"Listen, then," he said, "for I won my way to the temple of Arveid, east of the sun and west of the moon, in the land beyond the north wind where the ground is frozen night and day. There I found the Tree Illthorn which bears neither fruit nor leaf, and there beside it lies the temple. There I learned the truth.

"The Vollings are wrong—but they are also right. The Tyrnings are wrong—but they are right, as well. And in the distant mountains of the north live the Hill Folk who were driven out of Tyrningsland long ago for their religion, and they are also wrong, and right."

He saw the astonishment on their faces, and someone said, *"Herra,* how can that be?"

He went on, "The Vollings believe that Arveid was a Goddess who brought the selva to us. The Tyrnings hold that she was a mortal woman sent to this earth with the selva, and that she died after two hundred years. The Hill Folk believe that Ragnarok was fought on this earth long ago, that the earth was made again, and that Arveid is the Sun.

"This is the truth—the Last Battle was fought on earth and the world ended, but it was another world from this. This earth we stand on is a haven to which our ancestors came centuries ago, bringing the selva with them from their own world.

"Arveid was mortal. It was she who led them here, in a great ship which sailed the heavens. And when she had shown them how to dwell here, she became immortal. Her name will live forever, as she does among the gods.

"But the selva was made by men and women like ourselves, by our own ancestors. It was grown and nourished on their world, and brought here by them to be their mainstay."

He lifted himself still higher, and the radiance around him seemed to increase until they could hardly bear to look at him.

"Go, then!" he cried. "Return to your homes and tell this

message to all the folk. As Arveid brought our ancestors here
in one ship, so must all of you give up your battling and join
together in one belief in which there are parts of all beliefs.
Mortal and Goddess, savior of humankind after the world's
end—as she was that One, so must we all become one."

He closed the visor of his helmet as he finished, raised an
arm in farewell and soared above them into the thin, pure,
upper air. He had done his best to bring them together, thinking perhaps it might have been better done, but it was all he
was capable of. What they would do, how the story would be
told, he could not guess, but if it was to have any effect at all
he could not return to them. He must vanish forever from their
sight. He found that he scarcely cared; his separation from the
world he knew was more final than he had imagined. He was
a stranger now.

There was a task for him still, one that seemingly had not
occurred to Budri: to find the lake where the kraken grew and
to destroy the creature utterly once and for all. But first, he
must return to the temple. There, he would find the only three
people in the world who by now knew what he knew and
could speak to him as equals. At least, he would not be utterly
alone.

He set his face to the northwest, to the ship that had
crossed heaven, and to exile.